Volume 1

by Tony Abbott

SCHOLASTIC INC.

New York Toronto London Auckland Sydney
Mexico City New Delhi Hong Kong Buenos Aires

The Hidden Stairs and the Magic Carpet, ISBN 0-590-10839-5, text copyright © 1999 by Robert T. Abbott. Illustrations copyright © 1999 by Scholastic Inc. Book design by Dawn Adelman.

Journey to the Volcano Palace, ISBN 0-590-10841-7, text copyright © 1999 by Robert T. Abbott. Illustrations copyright © 1999 by Scholastic Inc. Book design by Dawn Adelman.

The Mysterious Island, ISBN 0-590-10840-9, text copyright © 1999 by Robert T. Abbott. Illustrations copyright © 1999 by Scholastic Inc. Book design by Dawn Adelman.

City in the Clouds, ISBN 0-590-10842-5, text copyright © 1999 by Robert T. Abbott. Illustrations copyright © 1999 by Scholastic Inc. Book design by Dawn Adelman.

12 11 10 9 8 7 6 5 4 3 2 1   5 6 7 8 9 10/0

Printed in the U.S.A.   40

This edition created exclusively for Barnes & Noble, Inc.

2005 Barnes & Noble Books

ISBN 0-7607-6482-4

First compilation printing, March 2005

Contents

The Hidden Stairs
and the
Magic Carpet

by Tony Abbott
Illustrated by Tim Jessell

For Dolores, Jane, and Lucy

One

The Small Room

Eric Hinkle ran past his mother on his way through the kitchen. He was heading to the back door.

"Neal and I are going to play soccer in the yard," he said. "Julie's coming, too. Gotta go."

"Stop." His mother blocked the door. "Didn't you forget something, Eric?"

She held out her hand.

She was holding empty garbage bags.

Eric looked at his mother. He looked at the garbage bags. All of a sudden, he remembered.

"Oh, no! I forgot about the basement!"

Knock, knock.

Eric sighed. He pulled the door open. Neal Kroger stepped into the kitchen. Neal lived at the end of Eric's street. He was Eric's best friend.

"Hey, what's up?" Neal asked.

"I have to clean the basement," Eric grumbled.

Mrs. Hinkle gave Eric the garbage bags. "You know your father wants to start remodeling the basement soon. This was supposed to be your special job."

Neal made a face at Eric. "That doesn't sound like much fun."

"According to my dad, it's not supposed to be fun," Eric replied. "It's supposed to be done."

"Give it two hours," Mrs. Hinkle said. She pointed to the clock. It was two o'clock.

"Two whole hours?" Eric headed for the basement door.

"Hey, I'll help," said Neal. "We'll be sort of a team. Maybe we'll find some cool stuff."

Eric smiled. Neal is a true friend, he thought. He'll even help clean up junk. "Okay. Come on."

Eric flicked on the light. The two boys tramped down to the basement.

On the right side of the stairs was the playroom. It had paneling on the walls, bookcases, a toy chest, a big sofa, and even a television.

"This looks pretty clean," Neal said, peeking in. "If my basement was like this, I'd live down here."

Eric liked the playroom, too. It was a great place to hang out on rainy days.

"The playroom isn't the problem," Eric said. "Look over here." He stepped into the other side of the basement. The room on the left side of the stairs. The side his father was going to remodel.

"What a mess!" Neal said, looking around.

On one wall was a tool bench filled with jars of nails, nuts, and bolts. On another wall were cabinets lined with canned food. An old washer and drier sat against a third wall.

And everywhere in between was junk. In piles. In bunches. In cartons. In boxes.

There was even a dusty old chair sitting in the middle of the floor.

"We'd better get started," Eric muttered.

Neal slumped into the old chair. "We? Did I say I would help?"

Eric stared at his friend. "You said we were a team."

"I'll be the coach," Neal said with a smile.

Tap, tap!

A face appeared at the basement window.

"It's Julie," said Eric. He waved. "Come in."

Julie Rubin had been friends with Eric and Neal ever since they got stuck in a tree together in kindergarten. Since then, they'd been in all the same classes. They even went to the same summer camp.

"Hi," Julie said as she raced down the stairs. She held a soccer ball under her arm.

"I thought we were going to play," she said, checking her watch. "It's only two o'clock."

Eric dragged a big toy box out from

under the stairs. "Sorry, I've got to clean all this stuff up."

"And I'm coaching," Neal said. "Ball, please?"

Julie passed the ball to Neal and looked around. "It looks like a big job. I'll help."

"How about a little game first?" Neal said. He stood up and bounced the ball once. Then he swung his foot hard. "Heads up, everybody!"

"Wait!" Eric yelled, ducking behind the box.

Too late. The ball was already in the air. It bounced off the tool bench and smacked Neal right in the face. "Ow! My nose!"

"Serves you right!" said Julie.

The ball bounced off the washing machine and rolled into the shadows by the stairs.

"I'll get it!" Julie jumped after the ball, then stopped. "Hey, what's this?" She

pointed to a door in the wall under the stairs. It was open slightly.

"My house has that, too," Neal said. "There's a cool little closet inside."

Eric remembered seeing that door a million times. But he had never been inside. "It must have swung open when I pulled that box away."

"Well, I think the ball went in there," Julie said. She swung the door open further. "Cool!"

Inside was a small closet. The ceiling was the underside of the basement stairs. It slanted all the way to the floor at the back of the room.

In the center sat the soccer ball.

"This is great," Eric said, peeking over Julie's shoulder. "We can put some of the junk in here."

Julie stepped into the room and reached

for the ball. "It's an awesome secret hide-out."

"Let me see!" Neal said. He jumped over to Eric, accidentally pushing him into the door.

Blam! It slammed shut.

A muffled scream came from inside the room.

"Help!" cried Julie. "I'm falling!"

Two

The Sky Below the Ground

Eric pulled the door open quickly.

Julie was standing in the middle of the tiny room. She was staring at the floor beneath her feet. The ball was nowhere in sight.

"Are you okay?" Eric asked.

Julie pushed her way quickly out of the room. "The ball went down there!"

Eric and Neal looked at the gray cement floor. Then they looked back at Julie.

"There were steps," Julie said. "And I almost fell all the way down!"

"Steps?" said Neal. "Where the floor is?"

Julie nodded. "And the soccer ball went bouncing down them. Then you opened the door, and the steps sort of . . . disappeared."

Eric and Neal entered the little room under the stairs. Then Julie stepped back in. They stood close together.

"Maybe the ball whacked you in the head, Julie," Neal said with a laugh. "You just thought there were stairs."

Eric looked down at the floor. There weren't any steps anywhere. "Julie, I don't think —"

"I'm not making this up," she said. "Wait. The door was closed. And it was dark at first. Maybe then . . ."

"It's pretty dark already," Neal said. "Don't close the door on us —"

Slam! Julie did close the door on them.

Neal grumbled. "Now it's very dark."

Then, suddenly, it wasn't.

The floor began to shimmer beneath them, and a bright light glowed under their feet.

Then — *whoosh!* — a stairway appeared out of nowhere. A set of steps, leading down. Leading away from the basement.

Away from the house.

"Whoa!" Eric said. "It looks like *outside* down there! Is this what you saw?"

Julie nodded. "Told you."

The steps glowed a rainbow of colors.

Julie peered over Eric's shoulder. "Let's go find the ball."

Neal reached for the door. "I don't think so."

"Come on," said Eric. He wasn't sure why, but he felt as if they had to go. He stepped down to the next step. Then to the next, and the next. Already the air was brighter where he was. It was pink. And cool and fresh.

"Neal. Julie. This is incredible," Eric said. "We have to go down."

"I don't think this is such a good idea," Neal said.

Julie laughed. She ran to catch up with Eric. "The air smells so sweet! Hurry up, Neal. We're already ten steps ahead of you."

Just below them was a forest of tall trees. The stairs led all the way down to the treetops.

"Unbelievable!" Eric whispered. "Do you think this is some kind of magic?"

"There's no such thing as magic," Julie said, biting her lip. She always did that when she didn't understand why things were happening. "But this place is beautiful. Strange, too. It's sort of like a theme park."

Eric stopped. What he saw coming out of the pink mist was not from any theme park he'd ever been to. "Uh-oh," he gasped.

"What do you see?" Neal asked.

Eric was frozen on the step, pointing into the mist. "Lizards, I think."

"In the trees?" Julie asked. "That's normal."

"No," Eric said. "Flying lizards. Big ones. With weird-looking red guys riding them . . ."

"That's not so normal," Neal said.

Thwang! A long, flaming arrow whistled past Eric's ear.

"Not so friendly, either! They're attacking us!"

Three

Groggles and Ninns

Thwang! Another arrow flew at them. Suddenly, flying lizards were everywhere. The riders on their backs were getting their bows ready for another shot.

"Run back up to my house!" Eric shouted.

"We can't!" Julie said. "The steps are disappearing. Look!" She pointed. The stairs were fading into the mist. Vanishing into the pink sky.

"Oh, man!" Neal cried. "I knew this would happen!"

Thwang! A third flaming arrow shot by.

"Follow me to the bottom," Eric yelled. "We can hide in the trees!" He rushed down, jumping two steps with every jump.

But the steps were disappearing under him.

"No!" he cried. He tumbled into the air.

"Ahhh!" Julie screamed.

Neal shouted, "Grab onto the —"

Eric didn't hear the rest. He fell like a rock through the trees. Branches snapped and cracked around him.

"Umph!" Eric moaned when he finally hit the ground. He lay there, facing the sky. For a second he couldn't remember where he was.

Then he saw the giant lizards circling lower.

Kaww! Kaww! They dived toward him.

"Holy cow!" Eric tried to crawl under a bush.

"Ouch! My ankle!" he groaned. He must have hurt it in the fall. He could hardly move.

The lizards swept even closer to the treetops. When they swooped, Eric saw the riders clearly. Their skin was as bright and shiny as red crayons!

"Oh, man, I must be dreaming!" he whispered to himself. "A really bad dream, too."

"It's bad," said a voice. "But it's no dream."

Eric turned his head. "Who said that?"

"Shhh!" Suddenly the bushes before him began to move, and someone leaped out at him.

It was a girl! She was dressed in a blue

tunic. A thick brown belt was wound around her waist.

Kaww! Kaww! The lizards swooped again.

The girl picked up a pebble. She threw it hard. It hit a distant tree with a loud *smack.*

"Over there!" cried a lizard rider, pointing to the tree. The lizards flew away.

"Whoa, cool move!" Eric looked into the girl's green eyes. Her skin was as pale as a cloud. "But . . . who are you?"

"Keeah," she said. "You must be from the Upper World. How did you get here?"

Eric blinked when he thought of how to tell her. "I . . . uh . . . sort of . . . fell."

"You picked the worst place in all of Droon. Lord Sparr is very close. His red Ninns are everywhere, hunting for me on their flying groggles."

"Lord Sparr?" Eric repeated. "Ninns? Groggles?"

"Did you hurt yourself?" The girl pressed her finger on Eric's ankle.

"Ouch!" Eric grunted.

"It's probably sprained." Then the girl opened a small leather pouch on her wrist. She sprinkled some sparkly dust on Eric's ankle. "Better?"

His leg began to tingle. He moved his foot.

"The pain's gone. How did you do that?"

"Never mind," the girl said. She began to scribble on a piece of paper. "You have to help me. Find Galen and tell him to send this message to my father, King Zello."

"King?" Eric repeated. "You're a princess?"

"There they are! Get them!" a voice cried out from above.

Fwap! Fwap! The lizards dived suddenly toward Keeah and Eric. They flapped to the ground and their red riders leaped off.

"The Ninns have spotted us!" Keeah cried. She pushed the wrinkled scrap of paper into Eric's hand. "Lord Sparr is a wizard. He's pure evil. He will stop at nothing to conquer Droon. Now, hurry. You'll find Galen in his tower."

"Tower?" said Eric. "I can't find any tower. I've got to find my friends and get home!"

The girl looked into his eyes. "If you're from the Upper World, you'll need help getting home. If you do this for me, I promise to help you. Now, I'll distract them while you go. Hurry!"

Without another word, Keeah leaped away swiftly, like a cat. The leaves fluttered above her, and Eric looked up. A strange white bird was gliding over the trees.

The bird seemed to be following her.

"There!" one Ninn yelled. "The princess!"

The red creatures broke branches and tore at leaves to get to Keeah. But she only ran faster.

"I don't believe any of this!" Eric said. He scrambled up from the ground and dashed down a narrow path after the princess. A stone bridge lay ahead of him. Maybe if he got there before the Ninns he could somehow help Keeah escape.

He had to try.

Eric raced toward the bridge.

"Get him!" cried a voice.

A hand came from nowhere.

It grabbed Eric.

It pulled him to the ground!

Four

At the Bridge

"Umph!" Eric rolled over and over until he stopped under the bridge. He looked up.

He couldn't believe his eyes.

"Neal! Julie! I thought I'd lost you — mmmf!"

Neal put his hand over Eric's mouth.

"Shhh!" Julie pointed to the top of the bridge. "Those ugly red guys are up there."

Eric nodded. Neal pulled his hand away.

Eric started speaking as quickly and as softly as he could. He told Neal and Julie what had happened to him.

"We're in someplace called Droon," he whispered. "I met a princess named Keeah. She gave me a message for her father, King Zello."

Neal glanced at the paper in Eric's hand, then gave him a strange look. "Uh-huh. Sure."

"The red guys are called Ninns," Eric continued. "We have to see what they're up to. Give me a boost!"

Neal grumbled but put out his hands so Eric could hoist himself up. A moment later, Julie was next to Eric. Together they peeked over the top of the bridge.

"Uh-oh," Julie whispered.

On the bridge were at least a dozen Ninns.

Up close, their red faces were puffy and

fat. Their slitty eyes were set close to-gether. Their chins were pointed. So were their ears.

On each hand were six clawed fingers.

"Lord Sparr will be angry!" one Ninn snarled.

"The girl's too quick!" snapped another. "And my groggle's too slow." He nodded at his lizard.

Ooga! Ooga! A sound like a horn blasted through the forest. Then the ground rum-bled.

"Is that a car?" Neal whispered from below.

"Uh . . . sort of," Julie answered.

But it wasn't like any car they had ever seen. It was long and yellow and had a bubble on top.

It bounced down the road on eight fat tires.

When it screeched to a stop in front of

the Ninns, a tall man stepped out. He was different from the others, Eric thought. He wasn't a Ninn.

His skin wasn't red, or pale like Keeah's.

He was human . . . pretty much. Well, except for two purple fins sticking up behind his ears.

"Where is the girl?" he snarled. His long black coat dragged heavily across the ground.

The Ninns trembled. One looked up. "The others helped her escape, Lord Sparr," he said.

Lord Sparr's eyes flashed in anger. And the fins behind his ears suddenly grew darker.

"Did you see that?" Julie whispered.

"He's some kind of wizard," Eric whispered back. "Princess Keeah said he was pure evil."

"How many others?" Sparr demanded.

Another Ninn held up his claw. He lowered three of his six fingers. "Three, my lord."

"Scour the forest! Burn it down if you must, but find the girl! Find her friends, too!" Lord Sparr turned and stormed back to his yellow car.

Ooga! Ooga! the horn blasted. The engine roared. The car tore away loudly down the road, leaving a cloud of thick blue smoke behind it.

Fwap! Fwap! The sound of flapping groggle wings filled the forest. A moment later, Eric and his friends were alone at the bridge.

"Lord Sparr is definitely bad news," Julie said. "And those ear fins are very weird."

"This whole place is weird, if you ask

me," Neal said. "How do we get out of here?"

Eric frowned. "Keeah said to find somebody named Galen who lives in a tower. If we do, she promised to help us get home. And Galen is also supposed to send this message to her father."

Eric unfolded the wrinkled paper Keeah had given him. In thin blue ink, it read,

Thginot Dekcatta Eb Lliw Frodnefroz

Eric scratched his head. "Well, this doesn't make any sense."

Julie laughed. "No kidding! I mean, flying lizards, bubble cars, a guy with fins on his head?"

"And all under your stairs," Neal added.

Eric didn't answer. He looked into the forest where he had last seen Keeah. He hoped she was safe. But something told him she wasn't.

"I think she's in danger," he said quietly.

"So are we," Julie added.

"Let's find this Galen guy," Neal said. "The sooner we do, the sooner we get home. There's a path this way. Come on."

Neal started running along the path.

He rushed into a clearing.

And he bumped his nose on something that wasn't there.

Five

The Vanishing Tower

"Oww!" Neal whined, cupping his hands over his face. Then he stared at the empty space in front of him. "Wait. I bumped into . . . nothing?"

Eric stood next to Neal and put his hands out. "No, there's something here. Something hard."

"Hard?" Neal grumbled. "Tell me about it."

"It's over here, too," Julie said as she walked to the other side of the clearing.

Eric went around the other way. "It's round. It must be some kind of — whoa!"

As the three of them stood there, a giant tower shimmered into view. A wooden tower. In fact, it was a tree. But when they touched it, the bark was as hard as stone.

"Hmm," Julie said, biting her lip. "This tree has petrified. It turned to stone because it's so old. We learned about petrified trees at camp."

"I don't remember that," said Neal.

"You were too busy eating snacks," Julie said.

"All that hiking made me hungry," Neal said.

"Guys!" Eric interrupted. "Can you please —"

"Who dares approach the tower of

Galen Longbeard!" cried a voice above them.

They all looked up and gasped.

Crawling slowly down the side of the tower was a large spider with eight long arms and legs. Only it wasn't an ordinary spider. It had a big, round face with large eyes and a pug nose.

And bright orange hair.

Neal nudged Julie. "I sure don't remember anything like *him* at camp," he whispered.

"You aren't Ninns!" the creature squeaked.

"Uh, that's true," Julie said. "Very true."

"In fact, the Ninns are after us," Eric said. "And we have a message from Princess Keeah."

"From the princess?" said the spider. "Then come inside quickly!"

Ploink! A door-sized section of the stony bark swung open.

"I'm Max, a spider troll," he said, jumping into the tree ahead of them. "We must go to the top!"

The three friends piled into the tree.

Together, they crawled up a winding passage and into a large, round room.

The room was cluttered beyond belief.

"Looks like your basement, Eric," Neal said.

Old leather books were stacked up everywhere. Hundreds of tiny colored bottles were collecting dust on deep wooden shelves. A big, ancient mirror leaned against one wall.

And in the center of everything stood a man.

He was tall and thin and very old. He wore a long blue robe and a high cone-shaped hat. His white beard hung down to his belt.

"Behold!" cried Max. "Galen Long-beard, first wizard of Droon! He's more than five hundred years old."

The old man coughed. "Yes, well, welcome to my tower," he said. Then he stroked his beard. "By the way, did anyone see Leep on the way up? Leep is my pilka."

"Uh, what's a pilka, sir?" Julie asked.

Galen cleared his throat. "Well, it's a . . . it has a . . . it goes like . . ." He waved his arms about, trying to describe the lost thing. "Oh, never mind. Leep will turn up somewhere. Now, what brings three Upper Worlders to my tower?"

Eric told Galen what had happened in the forest.

"Here is Keeah's message." Eric handed

the paper to Galen. "It doesn't make sense to us."

The wizard frowned. "Nor to me. Hmm . . ."

"I was thinking," Julie said, looking at the message again. "Maybe it's code. So if the Ninns captured us, they wouldn't understand it."

Galen laughed. "Princess Keeah knows that the Ninns are quite simple. Brains like walnuts. You might even say they are backward."

"Backward?" Neal said. "That's it! I bet Keeah's message is written backward. My sister tries that all the time. But she can't trick me!"

Neal scribbled out the message again, reversing the order of the letters from front to back.

"So . . ." he said. "'Thginot Dekcatta Eb Lliw Frodnefroz' becomes 'Zorfendorf

Will Be Attacked Tonight.' Does that make sense?"

Galen's eyes flashed suddenly. "Zorfendorf Castle! Lord Sparr plans to attack it tonight. I must warn King Zello immediately!"

Before another word was spoken, a blue mist rose around the wizard. Sparks of light streaked through it. Then he mumbled strange sounds.

"Kolo . . . bembo . . . zoot!"

An instant later — *zamm!* He wasn't there!

"Whoa!" Eric gasped. "Where did he —"

But — *zamm!* — Galen was already back. "I've just been to Jaffa City," he said. "King Zello is sending his army to defend Zorfendorf Castle."

"Mission accomplished!" Max chirped. "Sparr is stopped — for the moment."

Galen turned to the children. He looked

grim. "You have entered a troubled world, my young friends. Tell me, how did you come to be here?"

Julie told him how she found the steps in the little room in Eric's basement.

Galen sighed deeply. "Ah, the enchanted staircase. I wondered when it would appear again."

Eric blinked. "So you know about the stairs?"

The wizard walked slowly to a globe of Droon standing against the wall. Half of the globe was dark, half light. He stared at it for a long time.

"Ages ago, Lord Sparr created the Three Powers," Galen said finally. "Objects of unimaginable might. Fearing he would use them to take over your world, I sealed the stairs that once joined our two realms."

"I didn't know we lived in a realm!" said Neal.

"Indeed you do," Galen said. "But now I am old. My ancient spells grow weak. That is why the stairs are visible once again."

"They faded after we came down," Julie said.

Max chittered excitedly. "Keeah can help you find them. She has powers!"

Eric remembered how the princess cured his sprained ankle. "Is Keeah a wizard, too?"

Before Galen could answer, a buzzing sound came from across the room. *Zzzzt!*

Everyone turned to the old mirror. The rippled surface was flickering with a strange glow.

"A big-screen TV!" Neal joked. "How many channels do you get on this thing?"

"I use it to keep watch over Droon," Galen said. He waved his hand, and a scene moved hazily across the surface of the glass. "Like me, this mirror is old. But with it I can see most of what happens." The wizard's eyes widened suddenly in fear. "Oh, dear!"

"What's the matter?" Julie asked.

Galen pointed at the scene coming onto the mirror. It showed a vast black castle.

"Plud!" he gasped.

"Lord Sparr's evil fortress!" Max chittered.

The mirror zoomed in on the fortress.

In the courtyard were two red Ninns. Between them was a girl, struggling to get free.

"It's Keeah!" Eric cried. "The Ninns must have captured her in the woods."

And now she was a prisoner of Lord Sparr!

Six

Home Must Wait

"The forbidden city of Plud," Max said. "The Ninns have taken Princess Keeah to Plud!"

Eric stared at the mirror. "She seems really afraid. What are we going to do?"

"We must go to her!" Galen said, pulling a large sword down from the wall. "Plud is an evil place. It is where Keeah's mother, Queen Relna, fought her last battle against Sparr."

Neal shivered. "You mean, she's dead?"

"She was never seen again," Galen said as he slid the sword into his belt. "But that is not the worst of it. Sparr now seeks from Keeah the Red Eye of Dawn. It is one of the Three Powers I told you about. It is a jewel that commands the forces of nature."

"Does Keeah have it?" Julie asked.

Galen grabbed a helmet from a shelf. "I do not know. Even Keeah doesn't know. To stop Sparr from using the Powers for evil, I cast them to the winds and charmed them to change their shapes. No one knows what they have become."

"But Sparr will stop at nothing to have them again!" Max chittered, scurrying toward the passage to the ground. "I fear for Keeah. Hurry!"

Zzzzt!

"Wait," Julie said, turning back. "The mirror."

The hazy glass showed a city of bright

towers as light and sunny as Plud was dark. In the distance, a black cloud of groggles was descending.

"Sparr has tricked us!" Galen boomed. "His Ninns are attacking Jaffa City! Oh, I hope the princess can defend herself against Sparr until I return. I must go to Jaffa this instant."

"Wait," said Eric, turning to his friends. "Keeah helped me in the forest. And she was going to get us home. Now she's in trouble. I mean, we *have* to help her."

"How can we get to Plud?" Julie asked Galen.

"Hey!" Neal yelled suddenly. He jerked back, tumbling over a stack of books and hitting the floor with a thud. "Something just licked me!"

"Leep?" cried Max. He sprang up and landed in midair. "The pilka! I'm sitting on her!"

Galen quickly pulled at the air under Max. As he did, a silken fabric seemed to collect in his hands. And a creature took shape in the room.

It was an animal the size of a horse. But with long white fur. And six legs. And a friendly face.

It looked like a shaggy camel.

"Pilkas are quite friendly," said Max. "And quite fast! Leep seems to like you, Master Neal."

Hrrrr! The creature whinnied loudly. She plodded to the passage door and turned her head back, as if beckoning the children to follow.

Eric looked around at his friends.

"We're running out of time," Julie said.

Neal nodded. "Plus, we're a team, right?"

Eric felt his heart begin to race. "I guess we're going to Plud!"

Seven

The Forbidden City

"Take Leep at once," Galen told Eric and his friends as they stood outside the tower. "And take this invisible cloak. It may come in handy."

"And take me!" Max twittered. "I may come in handy, too. Besides, I know the way to Plud."

Galen smiled. "Good luck, my young friends, and remember what I am about to tell you. Droon is a secret to your world.

When you return home, tell no one about us. Also, you must not take anything from Droon with you, nor leave anything from the Upper World behind."

"Why?" Eric asked.

"For every object left here, a thing from Droon will appear in your world," the wizard replied.

"And it may not be a good thing!" Max added.

Neal blinked. "You mean like . . . a Ninn?"

"Or worse," Galen said. "Now I must go to Jaffa City and you to Plud. Be careful!"

Then, without another word — *zamm!* — Galen Longbeard, first wizard of Droon, vanished.

And his tower vanished with him.

Hrrr! The shaggy pilka whinnied.

"Well, what are we waiting for?" said Eric.

With the three children on her back and Max sitting on her head, Leep galloped out of the forest. She rode across open meadows while the pink sky darkened into late afternoon. It grew colder as the light faded.

A shape moved across the sky above them.

"Groggles?" said Julie.

Neal looked up. "No," he said. "A falcon. A white one. I think I saw it before, too. I remember falcons from our zoo trip last year."

Eric watched the bird soar away. "This one was in the forest when we first saw Sparr."

Hrrr! Leep whinnied sharply and slowed her gallop.

"Hush now," Max whispered. "We are close."

He pulled the reins, and the pilka plodded up a low hill to a jagged ridge.

The high black walls of a large city loomed before them. The sky was thick with clouds. The air smelled of smoke.

"Let me guess," Neal said. "This is Plud."

The three riders slid to the ground in a grove of trees. Max jumped down with Leep's cloak. "Don't forget this. Invisibility might be useful."

"So would a magic key," Julie said. "Those walls are super high. How do we get in?"

Rrrr! The ground began to rumble.

"A car?" Eric whispered. "Yes, Sparr's car! The gates will open for him. He's our way in!"

Ooga! Sparr's car roared loudly up the road.

Hrrr! The pilka reared, spooking at the sound.

"Leep, wait!" Max shouted. But the animal broke away from him. He scurried down the hill after her. "Leep! Leep!"

"Come back, Max," Julie said. "We need you!"

The car roared by. The gates of Plud opened.

"We're losing our chance," Eric hissed. "Come on!" He grabbed Neal and Julie.

The three of them dashed in after the yellow car. They jumped behind a low wall just as — *chong!* — the huge black gates closed.

Sparr's car screeched to a stop in a courtyard. A group of Ninns raced out to greet their master.

"The princess is in the main tower," one said.

Without a word, Sparr stomped into the fortress. The Ninn guards marched in after him.

"Okay," Eric whispered. "Let's go. Quietly."

They slipped into the fortress. The hallways were as narrow and dark as the streets outside. Ninn footsteps echoed loudly on the stone floors.

Julie stopped. "Wait. Do we have a plan?"

Eric peered into the dark. "There are some steps ahead. If we sneak up to the main tower, maybe we can get to Keeah before Sparr does."

Neal nodded. "And get back out, too. Right?"

"Of course," Eric said.

"Sounds good," said Julie. "Lead on."

They tiptoed up the long stairway. After what seemed like hundreds of steps they reached the top of the main tower. At the end of a short hallway was a door. Two big Ninns in black armor guarded it.

"Do we have to . . . fight them?" Neal whispered, out of breath.

Eric shook his head. "No. Now we use some magic." He pulled Galen's cloak over himself.

"I like it," Julie said. "Poof, you're gone!"

"Hide in the shadows," Eric said. Then, completely invisible, he slipped down the hall.

He jabbed one of the guards in the shoulder.

"Stop that!" the Ninn yelled. He swatted the other Ninn in the arm.

"I didn't do anything!" the second Ninn cried. He whacked the other on his shiny black helmet.

"I'll get you for that!" the first Ninn yelled.

"Not if I get you first!" the other growled, butting the first one on the head and chasing him right past the kids and down the stairs!

A moment later, the hallway was clear.

"Great job!" Julie said as Eric pulled off the cloak and looped it around his belt.

"I'll stand guard outside," Neal said. "You two go in and get the princess."

Eric and Julie unbolted the door and pushed it open. They entered a small, dark room.

Princess Keeah was sitting on the floor. She looked up and jumped. "The boy in the woods!"

Eric grinned. "We've come to rescue you!"

Keeah smiled. "I knew someone would come." Then her smile faded. "But if we're going to get out of here at all, we need to hurry!"

As quickly as she had run through the forest, Keeah scampered from the room and down the hallway. Eric, Julie, and Neal followed her.

"Sparr thinks I have the Red Eye of Dawn," Keeah whispered. "With it, he plans to conquer all of Droon!"

"And so I shall, Princess Keeah!"

The four children froze in the dark hall.

Out of the shadows stepped Lord Sparr.

Eight

Prisoners!

Clomp! Clomp! The children were marched to a room at the top of another tower. A dozen Ninn warriors in shiny black armor surrounded them.

Clang! The iron door was bolted shut. They were prisoners.

Lord Sparr paced back and forth before a thick blue curtain that covered one of the walls.

"Princess Keeah," he began. "You and

your friends spoiled my plans to attack Zorfendorf Castle. And Galen discovered my little raid on Jaffa City. No matter. Having *you* as a prisoner is far more valuable. Besides, you have something that belongs to me."

The princess backed away. "Let us go, Sparr. My father is on his way here right now."

Sparr laughed. "Neither your father nor your mother will ever see you again."

"My mother died," Keeah said. "And my —"

The sorcerer smirked. "Your mother is —" Then he stopped. His eyes flashed. "That leather pouch on your wrist . . ."

"What?" Keeah said.

Sparr grabbed the pouch from Keeah.

"My mother gave me that!" she cried, trying to take it back.

But Sparr held it high. His fins turned

inky black. He began to shake. "O jewel, if it be you, show me now your shape so true!"

At once, the pouch began to shrink in Sparr's palm. It shriveled to the size of a small egg.

Then it turned very smooth.

Then it turned red.

It began to glow.

"No . . ." Keeah gasped. "No . . . no!"

Sparr howled. "The Red Eye of Dawn! You had it all along! Now I have it. The First Power is mine once again!"

"Give it back to her, you smelly fish head!" Eric yelled. He rushed at Sparr, but one of the Ninns grabbed him and pushed him roughly into Julie and Neal. Then the sorcerer spoke words that made their blood turn to ice.

"I . . . know . . . you . . . three. . . ."

"What?" Julie said. "How could you —"

"You are from the Upper World. You

have found the stairs. *My* stairs." Sparr pointed at Eric. "They are . . . in your house!"

Eric shuddered. "How do you know that?"

"I know many things about you," Sparr said. Then he reached back and tore the blue curtain aside.

"Uh-oh," Neal whispered.

Behind the curtain was a tall display stand. On the stand was a round black-and-white object.

"Our soccer ball!" Julie exclaimed.

"I have learned much from this object," Sparr said, hovering over the ball. "But not as much as I shall learn . . . when I am done with you."

Suddenly, a voice cried shrilly from the window. "You are done right now, Sparr!"

Everyone turned to see a mop of orange hair scurry down the wall.

"Max!" Julie cried.

"The one and only!" Max jumped to the floor and quickly spun a sticky web of threads around the Ninns' feet. "Ha-ha!" he chittered.

"G-g-g-guards!" Lord Sparr sputtered. "Take them all to the dungeon!"

His red warriors lunged at the children.

And tripped on Max's gooey web!

"All right!" Eric cried, leaping for the soccer ball and tossing it high. "Neal! Your famous bad kick! Just like in my basement!"

Neal grinned. "Heads up, everybody!" He jumped at the ball and kicked it hard.

"Akkk!" One Ninn groaned. "My nose!"

"Serves you right!" Julie shouted. She snuck up and kicked the ball again. This time, it went straight for another Ninn's stomach. He fell back into two others, knocking them to the floor.

"Score!" Eric said, diving for the ball.

"I'll get the Red Eye of Dawn!" Keeah cried.

But Sparr spun around and raised his fist.

Kla-blam! A bolt of red fire shot from his hand. He staggered backward as the fire blew past Keeah, punching a hole straight through the wall to the hall outside.

"We'll get the Eye later!" Eric shouted. "Everybody out!" He jumped through the hole in the wall with Neal and Keeah. Julie and Max ran after them. They all rushed down the hall.

But the Ninns were right on their heels.

"This way!" said Eric, tumbling through a narrow door. He tossed the soccer ball to Julie and slammed the door behind them.

"Uh-oh," said Neal as he looked around.

Dim light from a high window showed that they were in a small room.

A very small room.

"Uh-oh is right," Julie said. "I think we found a dungeon all by ourselves!"

Nine

Into Thin Air!

Wham! Wham! The Ninns battered the door, but Eric and Neal held it as tight as they could.

"Dungeons don't have exits," Max said, crawling to the window. "This is a storage room."

"Too bad it's not a *magic* storage room," Julie said. "The invisible cloak isn't big enough for all of us. And there's nothing here but these dumb old rugs."

"Rugs?" said Keeah. "They might be old, but . . . maybe they're not so dumb. Check the label."

Clonk! The Ninns banged harder on the door.

Julie read the label. "It says, 'Rugs by Pasha. Do not remove this tag.'"

Keeah's face lit up. She nearly laughed. "Find a green one with purple spirals in the corners."

"This is no time to pick out a rug!" Eric said.

"Not just any rug," Keeah said. "A Pasha original." She helped Julie tug out one big carpet. They spread it on the floor.

Kkkrrkk! The door started to splinter.

Eric felt his strength slipping away. "We can't hold this door much longer!"

"Everyone on!" Keeah said, sitting on the rug.

Julie jumped on. "Now what? We fly?"

Suddenly, the carpet lifted from the floor.

"Yikes!" Julie gasped. "I guess we do!"

Keeah laughed. "The carpet must like your voice. Pasha's rugs don't fly for just anybody."

Julie shrugged. "All I said was . . . fly."

Swoosh! The carpet circled the room!

Blam! The door shook. One of its hinges blasted off.

Max strained with his thin arms and pried the window open. Cold air swirled in from outside.

"Max! Eric! Neal!" Julie cried. "Get on the rug!"

"No," said Max. "I must go save Leep. Besides, I don't ride rugs. I get airsick, you know!"

Waving with three of his arms, Max scrambled out the window and down to the ground below.

Neal jumped onto the rug, holding the soccer ball between his legs. "Whoa! It's wobbly up here!" He clung to the long fringe and held out a hand to Eric. "Grab on, pal!"

Kkkrunch! The door burst open, and a dozen Ninns rushed in, with Lord Sparr in the lead.

Eric leaped to the carpet.

"I *will* stop you!" Sparr cried. He thrust his fist at them. "Red Eye of Dawn, give me the power!"

Kla-bbblam! Bolts of jagged fire exploded in the room just as the carpet slid out the window.

The rug pulled away into the air. But Sparr aimed his fist again.

"He's going to blast us!" Neal yelled.

Suddenly, the white falcon was there, tearing out of the clouds! It swooped with incredible speed, right at Sparr.

"It's attacking him!" Keeah cried.

Ka-whoom! The flame from the red jewel seemed to engulf Sparr's hand. He stumbled back, his face twisted in pain, as the fiery bolts flew harmlessly into the air.

"Missed by a mile!" yelled Julie. She steered the rug higher and higher into the sky.

"I will hunt you down!" Sparr shouted. But the falcon swooped again, driving him back from the window.

Swoosh! The carpet lifted up from the fortress.

"Yahoo!" Eric yelled as they soared into the sky.

He was still yelling when they disappeared behind the clouds.

Ten

The World Under the Stairs

Swoosh! Swoosh!

Pink air swirled all around the flying carpet.

"We did it! We're free!" cried Keeah. She looked over the side until Plud was a tiny dot on the ground. Then she turned to Eric.

"Thank you. You helped me, even though you didn't know me. Now let me get you home."

Eric scanned the distance. "The magic

stairs faded. I don't know where they are now."

"I saw them in a dream once," Keeah said, narrowing her eyes. "They were in the ice hills of Tarabat. Let's try there. Julie, head north!"

Julie pulled hard, and the rug swept upward.

As they flew, snow began to swirl in the air. Cold winds howled over them. A few minutes later, they were swerving through narrow mountain passes and over icy peaks.

Suddenly, a rainbow of colors glistened ahead of them.

"There it is!" cried Neal. "We found it!"

Julie tugged a fringe. The carpet dipped toward the hills. It slowed and hovered at the foot of the stairs.

The three friends hopped to the bottom step.

Eric turned to Keeah. "Galen was right. We did enter a world in trouble."

Keeah nodded. "But a world with hope, too. Thanks to all of you, I can keep fighting Lord Sparr."

Eric handed her Galen's invisible cloak. "Galen said we can't take anything with us."

Keeah smiled. She held the soccer ball in her hands for a moment, then tossed it to Eric. "And don't leave anything behind!"

Then she tugged on the carpet. Obediently, it pulled away from the steps.

"Will we see you again?" Eric called out.

The icy air began to sing all around Keeah. "If the magic works, you will!"

A moment later, she soared over the hills.

Eric stared into the snowy air until she was gone. "If the magic works?"

"Better hurry," Julie said, starting up the steps, "or we'll be stuck in this snowstorm forever."

The three friends ran up the stairs and entered the small room in Eric's basement.

Eric turned to take one last look at the strange world of snow beneath them.

"Good-bye, Droon," he said. He touched the wall next to him. *Click!* The light went on.

The cement floor instantly took shape beneath them. The world under the stairs disappeared.

As if it had never existed.

The three friends just stared at one another for a long time. Finally Eric opened the door and walked out into the basement. It was still cluttered and messy.

"I don't know," he said, dropping the soccer ball onto the dusty chair. "It does seem kind of impossible, doesn't it?"

"Oh, yeah?" Neal said, holding his stomach. "I still feel that rug bouncing under me."

"And we helped Keeah," Julie said. "That was real. It was too cool *not* to be real!"

Eric slid a box in front of the door. "Galen told us to keep Droon a secret. And Keeah said we'll know we're going back, 'if the magic works.' Until then, I guess we just have to wait."

Julie checked her watch. "We've been gone for hours. We'd better tell our parents we're okay."

Together they tramped up to the kitchen. Eric took a deep breath and opened the door.

His mother was sitting at the dinner table. She had a shocked look on her face. "Eric?"

"Mom, let me try to explain. We —"

"Eric," she said, "you'll never get the job done if you give up so soon." She pointed to the clock.

It was only ten minutes after two.

"We did all that *in ten minutes?*" Neal said.

Julie's mouth dropped open. "That means —"

Mrs. Hinkle stood up. "You've finished the entire basement?" She started for the door.

"Mom, no!" Eric said, blocking the door. "Actually, we didn't get far. There's still a lot to do."

She glared at him. "Because after the basement is the attic. And the porch. And the garage —"

Wham! The basement door slammed shut as Eric and his friends rushed back down the stairs.

They stopped at the bottom and stared.

Floating silently in the middle of the messy room was the soccer ball. Across the surface of the ball were letters written in thin blue ink.

Nruter Ot Uoy Llet Lliw Smaerd Ruoy

"A message from Keeah!" Eric cried.

Neal studied the words. "It says, 'Your dreams will tell you to return.'"

Suddenly, the patches of black and white swirled across the surface of the soccer ball, forming the ragged shapes of countries.

"It's a globe," said Julie. "A globe of Droon!"

The globe floated magically for a few moments, then changed back into a ball again.

It dropped into Eric's hands.

"Whoa!" he gasped. "Guys, I'm no wiz-

ard, but I'm pretty sure the magic is working!"

"Me, too," said Neal. "I say we go home
tonight and do some serious dreaming!"

Julie nodded. "And we keep on dreaming —"

"— until we get back to Droon!" Eric
said.

Then the three friends laughed out loud
together.

"To Droon!" they cheered.

Journey
to the
Volcano Palace

by Tony Abbott
Illustrated by David Merrell

To Mrs. Schwarz
and her wonderful class of
wizards in training

One

Dreams

Eric Hinkle couldn't breathe.

The air around him was dark and smoky and hot. The evil sorcerer Lord Sparr was after him, chasing him down a long, dark tunnel.

"Now that you know my secret," Sparr shouted, "you will never be able to leave!"

"I don't know any secret!" Eric pleaded. "Let me go! Let me out of Droon!"

"NEVER!" was Sparr's only word.

The sorcerer's eyes were filled with anger. The weird fins behind his ears were purple and shiny. He was getting closer. Closer!

The tunnel ahead of Eric split in two.

Go right! said a voice in his head.

"Oh, man!" Eric swallowed hard. He had always had a problem with right and left. He looked at his hands. Which was right? It took him a second to decide. "This way!" he said.

He charged ahead into one of the tunnels.

No! said the voice in his head. *The right one!*

"Ha! Now I have you!" Sparr shrieked as Eric ran up against a solid wall. "My secret is safe!"

"Help!" Eric cried. "I'm trapped!"

Sparr lunged.

Eric leaped out of the way.

Thud!

"Ouch!" Eric groaned.

He opened his eyes. He was in his room. He was half on the floor, half still in bed, wound up tight in his bedsheet. He looked like a mummy.

"Whoa!" he said. "What a nightmare."

The door opened. His mother stood in the doorway. "Eric, what was that noise?"

"Uh, I guess I fell out of bed," Eric said, unwinding himself from his sheet. "But I'm okay."

Mrs. Hinkle helped him up. "By the way, Eric. Where is Droon?"

Eric nearly fell to the floor again. "Huh?"

"You were talking in your sleep," his mother said. "Something about a place called Droon."

Eric gulped. He blinked. His mouth opened to answer, but nothing came out.

Droon was a secret. No one was supposed to know about the incredible world he and his friends had found under his basement stairs.

Galen the wizard had made them promise not to tell anyone.

The problem was, ever since his first time in Droon, Eric couldn't think of anything else.

Now he was even *dreaming* about it.

And Princess Keeah had told them that when you dreamed about Droon, it meant you would go back.

"Uh, Droon is a place we, uh . . . made up," Eric said. "Neal and Julie and I."

He hated to lie. But until he and his friends found out more about Droon — and about the evil Sparr — it wasn't safe for people to know.

"Sounds secret," his mother said. "By the way, your friends called. They're coming over."

Eric dressed quickly. He had to tell Neal and Julie about his dream right away.

He got to the backyard in time to see a small, scruffy dog chasing Neal across the lawn.

Grrr! The dog kept biting Neal's feet.

"Stop it, Snorky!" Neal tossed a biscuit across the yard. The dog bounced after it. "Hey, Eric."

"I'm glad you're here," Eric said. "It happened. I had a weird dream about Droon —"

"Not me." Neal shook his head. "I was so tired teaching Snorky to fetch, I fell asleep before I hit the pillow. Actually, I fell asleep on my floor."

"I woke up on the floor!" Eric said. "It

was weird. It felt like someone from Droon was *sending* the dream to me."

At that moment, Julie came into the yard.

Eric ran over to her. "Julie, something strange is going on —"

"First, let me tell you about my dream," Julie said. "I was in Droon —"

"Me, too!" Eric gasped. "Sparr was chasing me because I knew his big secret. But I forget what the secret was."

"Hmm." Julie bit her lip. She always did that when she was trying to figure something out. "I was at a pool of water. I was really thirsty and I wanted to take a drink, but something creeped me out. I forget what it was, but it was very yucky."

Grrr! Snorky ran back across the lawn. He fastened his teeth on the toe of Neal's right sneaker.

"Let go of my shoe!" Neal cried. "Wait a

second. . . . I remember now. I had a scary dream, too! I forget most of it, except . . ."

"Except for what?" Julie asked.

Neal shrugged. "I remember it was about my feet. I was in Droon, and my feet hurt."

Snorky leaped suddenly for Neal's left shoe.

"Heel!" Neal snapped, shaking his foot.

"Well, he's *eating* your heel," Julie said.

"Maybe he's learning!" Neal tossed another biscuit, and Snorky ran for it. "Let's get inside."

The three kids jumped up the back steps into Eric's kitchen and headed for the basement.

"Droon is full of secrets," said Julie. "Secrets we need answers to. We need to go back."

Neal frowned. "But what if all of our dreams come true? I mean, my dream was pretty weird."

"There's only one way to find out," said Eric.

They tramped down the stairs into the basement. It was messy. It was beyond messy. Eric knew he'd have to clean it one of these days.

Cleaning all the old toys and junk out of the basement was his special project. Neal and Julie had said they would help.

When we get back, Eric thought.

He pulled open the little door under the stairs. They entered a small, empty room.

They closed the door. They all held their breath as Eric switched off the light.

Whoosh! The floor vanished beneath them.

In its place was a long flight of stairs. The steps shimmered in the light from below.

The light from the land of Droon.

"Yes! We *are* going back," Eric whispered. "I wonder where the stairs will lead us this time."

"Or if it's day or night in Droon," said Neal.

"Let's stop talking and find out," said Julie.

The three friends stepped slowly down the stairs. The air was hushed and cool. And the sky below them turned deep blue and sparkled like a million jewels.

A giant moon cast golden light on the stairs.

"Nighttime," Eric whispered.

Before they knew it, the three friends were in Droon once again.

Two

Sands of Time

A wide sea of sand stretched away as far as the eye could see. Sand hills — dunes — rolled and dipped all the way to the horizon.

"Wow!" Neal said. "This is my first desert."

The moonbeams made the dunes glitter with golden light.

"This is awesome," Julie said. "Droon is beautiful at night."

Eric breathed in the cool air. "Let's climb over that dune," he said, pointing to one of the high, curving hills of sand. "For a look."

They stepped down from the bottom step.

The sand was warm.

They climbed to the top of the dune and peered over.

Not far away was a striped tent. Shaggy, six-legged beasts stood outside. The kids remembered them from their first time in Droon. The beasts were called pilkas.

"Somebody's camping," Neal whispered.

Eric noticed a strange purple flag flying over the tent. "Careful," he said. "You never know what you might find."

"We don't have much choice," said Julie, pointing behind them. "The stairs are fading."

The three friends watched as the rainbow-colored steps vanished in the sky.

"I hope we find them again later," Neal said. "Wherever they are."

Slowly, they approached the tent. A large flap hung down over an opening.

"Let's peek in," Julie whispered.

Suddenly, a voice spoke from inside the tent. "Come in!"

Julie held her breath and pulled up the flap.

The three friends looked inside.

Their friend Princess Keeah was sitting on a rug spread out over the sand. She was dressed in a light blue tunic. In her long blonde hair she wore a golden crown.

Next to her sat the old wizard, Galen Longbeard, and his assistant, Max.

Lining the inside of the tent were piles of extra-plump purple-colored pillows.

"Welcome back!" Keeah said, laughing when she saw the kids.

"We've all been waiting for you!" Max

chirped happily. Max was a spider troll. He had eight legs and could spin sticky webs and climb up walls. But his face was pudgy like a troll's, and his bright orange hair sprouted straight up.

Eric smiled as he and his friends entered the tent. "How did you know we were coming?"

"I can see the future!" Keeah said.

Julie gasped. "You can?"

"Keeah," said Galen sternly, "you must respect your real magic powers. You should not invent others you don't have . . . yet."

The princess made a face. "I'm sorry." She turned to the three friends. "Actually, I can't see the future. I just dreamed about all of you, and I guessed you were on your way."

Eric shot looks at Julie and Neal. "We had dreams, too. But we didn't understand them."

"In Droon, wizards — and sorcerers — can use dreams as messengers," Galen said. "Sometimes they foretell what will happen. We may understand more at dawn, when we begin —"

Neal tugged a purple pillow over to the rug.

"Hey!" the pillow snarled. "You pinched me! I was having the nicest nap, too!"

Neal jumped up. "Whoa . . . sorry!" He looked around. "Wait, did that pillow just talk to me?"

Max chirped in laughter. "That's a Lumpy!"

Neal made a face. "Lumpy or not, in the Upper World, pillows don't talk!"

Keeah smiled. "Max means it's not a pillow you sat on. It's a Lumpy. A purple Lumpy!"

It was then that the kids noticed small round faces on the chubby pillows. Their cheeks bulged, and their noses were like purple tennis balls.

One of the creatures stood up, stretched, and yawned. It had short, fat arms and squat legs.

"I am Khan," he said. "King of the purple Lumpies of Lumpland. Just over the last dune on your left. We Lumpies are the best desert trackers in Droon. We sniff out trouble." He paused to sniff the air. "Danger is everywhere!"

"Uh . . . pleased to meet you!" Eric said.

Galen rose, wrapping his long blue robe around him. "Now, come outside. We must talk about tomorrow."

The air outside the tent was cool and sweet.

"It sure is peaceful here," Julie said.

"It wasn't yesterday," Keeah told them. "That's the reason we're here."

"What happened?" Eric asked.

"Lord Sparr," Khan said, shaking his purple fist in the air. "He nearly destroyed one of our villages with his red jewel. Luckily, the terrible flame burned his hand, and he fled."

Eric remembered the red jewel. It was called the Red Eye of Dawn. The sorcerer Sparr had stolen it from Keeah and was planning to use it to take over Droon.

"The Eye of Dawn commands the forces of nature," Galen said. "Fire, wind, wave, and sky. It is *very* powerful. Yesterday, Droon was lucky. Tomorrow, we may not be."

Keeah pointed across the desert. "We think Sparr fled to his secret palace. It's in a hidden land called Kano."

Galen turned grim. "A terrible place, dangerous and deadly. Sparr will not expect us to go."

Neal nodded. "We'd be dumb to do that."

"And because he doesn't expect it," Keeah added, "that's exactly what we'll do!"

The three kids were silent.

Eric blinked. "Dangerous and deadly?"

Khan nodded. "And the Lumpies shall lead you right to it!"

"We must find the Eye before Sparr uses it again," Galen said. "Droon itself is at stake."

"Are you in?" Keeah asked.

Eric looked at Julie, then at Neal. He knew they were just as afraid as he was.

"I guess we're in," Julie said.

"Get the maps," Neal said. "I'd like to see exactly where we're going."

Max chuckled. "Maps will be of no help! Lord Sparr lives in a volcano!"

Three

The Oasis at Noon

Moments later, the sun began to rise over the distant dunes.

"It's time!" Keeah said.

They all climbed to the rim of a tall, curving sand dune. Galen pointed to the sandy plains where the sun was rising.

"The door to Kano lies in the East," the wizard said. "According to a legend, it can be seen where it is not."

Eric nodded slowly. "Okay. Got it. Great. Um . . . could you say that again?"

"It's a riddle," Max said, scurrying back and forth in the sand. "No one knows exactly where Sparr's palace is."

Julie began biting her lip again. "Then how are we going to find the door to Kano?"

But Galen was already walking back down the dune. "By finding the answer to the riddle!"

"First things first," Khan said. "Our journey of many miles begins with a single sniff!" He sniffed the air, then pointed. "East is that way!"

Within moments, Khan and his Lumpies packed up the tent and supplies.

"Into the East!" Max chirped.

Hrrr! Galen's shaggy pilka, Leep, whinnied in excitement as the kids piled onto her back.

"We're off!" cried Julie.

They rode for hours over the hot dunes.

Mile after mile, they saw nothing but burning white sand.

"I think we're lost," Neal said, wiping his forehead. "I mean, I guess we're in the East, but I don't see any doors. All I see are two things. Sand, and more sand."

Eric pointed into the distance. "What's that?"

It looked like a shadow against the far-away dunes, a grove of trees waving in the breeze.

"Is it a mirage?" Julie said. "You know, the imaginary things you see in the desert that aren't really there?"

"Imaginary," Eric sighed. "Right now I'm imagining the town pool filled with cool water."

"You want water, you got it," Neal said.

"I'm gonna be a puddle in about three minutes."

"No, you won't," Keeah said. "That's an oasis! We can rest there and get some real water!"

They rode quickly and soon reached a group of tall palm trees sprouting up from the dunes.

In the center was a pool of cool, blue water.

Eric and his friends slid down from Leep and moved into the shade of the waving palm trees.

"This isn't the pool in my dream," Julie said. "There's nothing yucky about this."

"Good!" Neal exclaimed. "Because I'm *way* past thirsty." He and Julie and Keeah went to the near side of the pool and began to drink.

The Lumpies led the pilkas over. They all bent their heads to the water.

"Drink up," Khan said. "It may be many miles before we find water again."

Eric scrambled to an open spot on the side of the pool. He breathed in the sweet air under the trees, then bent down, cupping his hands together. The shimmering water looked so refreshing.

He stooped to take a big sip.

He froze solid at what he saw.

"What is it?" Keeah said, looking up.

Eric stared into the pool. "My reflection —"

Neal laughed. "Yeah, you look pretty grimy!"

"We all do," Julie added.

"No, that's not it," Eric mumbled. In the surface of the pool he saw his face. Behind his head were the tops of the palm trees that he knew were waving in the wind behind him.

And behind the palm trees . . . was an

enormous gate! A gate made of black iron, towering up behind the palms.

Eric whirled around and looked up.

There was no gate behind the palm trees.

He turned back to the pool. The gate was there, in the reflection, standing as huge and as plain as day!

"An invisible gate!" he gasped. "Like the riddle says — it can be seen where it is not!"

"What?" Neal said, slurping from his hands.

"We're here!" Eric cried. "I see it in the pool. The door to Kano. But it's *not* in the pool. It's *there*!" He pointed up behind him, beyond the palm trees. "The entrance to Kano is right there!"

Galen rushed over. Max scurried across the sand. Keeah, Neal, and Julie ran to Eric.

They all stared at the open air behind the palms, then at the pool.

"It's there, all right," Keeah said. "But it's still invisible. How do we get in?"

"I have an idea." Neal stooped to the pool and filled his hands with water. He hurried through the palm trees to where the gates would be.

He tossed the water across the air.

Sssss! The water struck something in midair and spilled down it.

Suddenly, there it was! A patch of black iron!

Julie tried it next.

Sssss! More of the black gate appeared.

Everyone joined in, even the Lumpies. They cupped their hands. They used buckets. They even filled their boots with water.

Splish! Splosh! Splursh!

Soon, the entire gate dripped into shape

before them. It stood huge and glistening behind the tall palm trees of the oasis.

Galen stood back in awe. "Behold! We have discovered the way to Sparr's secret realm! This is the door to Kano!"

Four

Into Sparr's Realm

The iron gate towered high above the dunes, casting its dark shadow over the oasis.

"Quickly! Quickly!" Khan shouted to the pilkas. The shaggy creatures nudged the black gate. Again and again they pushed against it.

Max sat on Leep's head, urging her on. "Hurry, the water is drying! The gate will disappear!"

Errr, errr! The giant door began to creak open.

"Yes!" Eric gulped. "We've done it."

Everyone slipped through.

Klang! The gate closed loudly behind them.

Right away, the air was hotter. It was hazy and brown and bad-smelling. Not clear and pinkish-blue like over the rest of Droon.

"We've entered Sparr's hidden empire," Max chirped. "This is the nasty land of Kano!"

"Stinky," Khan mumbled to his fellow Lumpies. "As I expected."

Galen nodded to himself and smiled as he looked around at the smoky brown air. "Yes, this is good. Very good!"

Neal coughed. "Excuse me, sir, but what's so good? This place is so smelly I can hardly breathe!"

"There are no Ninns at the gate," the

wizard replied. "That means that Lord Sparr does not yet know we are here. But we must hurry."

They climbed back on the pilkas and rode ahead. Before long the small band found itself standing on a steep ridge. A sudden wind swept across them. The dark air cleared for a second.

They stood above a deep, black valley.

The ground was dark and burnt for miles. It was easy to see the reason why. In the middle of the valley was a giant black cone.

It looked like a tall mountain, except that its top was torn open. And a huge pool of lava splashed and spurted and bubbled in the middle.

"A volcano!" Julie gasped.

"That is the heart of Kano, the black mountain home of Lord Sparr," Galen told them. "Come."

The wizard galloped into the lead. Max clung to his pilka's mane, while Leep, with the children on her back, trotted alongside. Khan and his purple Lumpies rode close behind them all.

They made their way quietly but quickly to the center of the valley.

"Maybe Sparr's not home," Neal whispered. "That would be pretty good."

"I hope Sparr *is* here," Keeah said as they rode closer. "I want to fight him as he fought my mother. Besides, wherever he is, the Eye is, too."

Neal, Eric, and Julie knew Keeah blamed Sparr for the disappearance of her mother, Queen Relna. Two years before, the queen had fought Sparr in a fierce battle. She was never seen again.

Galen spurred his pilka quickly to the mountain. "Khan and I will scout for the entrance to the volcano palace. In the meantime — beware of fire monsters!"

Neal blinked and looked at Julie. "Did he say *fire* monsters?"

Eric clambered up onto a long, crusted rock that lay in front of the mountain. "Maybe the entrance is behind these big stones."

"What do you see?" Keeah called out.

"Not much," Eric said. "Wait, there *is* an opening! We can go in — hey! This rock just moved!"

"Uh, I don't think it's a rock," Julie said, pointing to a big green eyeball flicking open just under Eric's foot. I think it's . . . it's . . . a monster!"

Hrooosh! A column of fire spurted from the beast's mouth, burning the black ground blacker.

"A fire monster!" Neal shouted.

Suddenly, another stony-gray shape shook itself. A large green eye opened on it, too. It thrust its head up into the air. *Hrooosh!*

"Two fire monsters!" Neal shouted.

Galen charged over. "Get inside!" he yelled to the children. Then he leaped onto the back of one monster and began wrestling with it.

"Lumpies, help the wizard!" Khan called out. Instantly his Lumpies jumped on the second monster. They pinched it and poked it with all their might.

"Max, Khan, lead the children through!" Galen shouted.

The stone-skinned monsters thrashed and twisted, but Galen and the Lumpies kept on fighting.

"We can't leave you!" Keeah cried.

"You must!" the wizard commanded. "Find the Eye! It is the only way to save —"

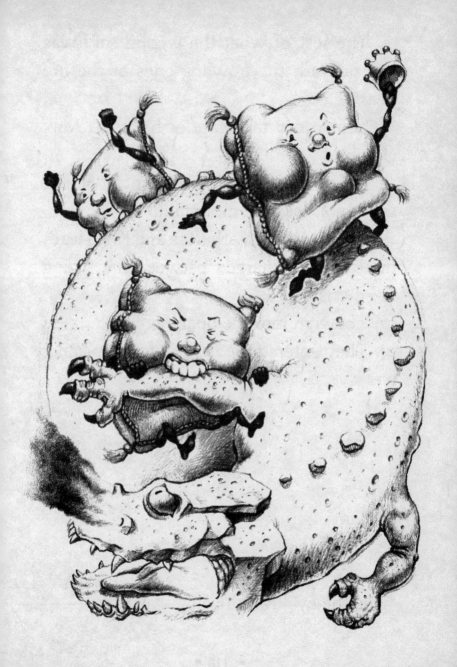

The rest of what the wizard said was lost beneath the howling cries of the fire beasts.

"Galen can take care of himself," Max chittered.

Khan rushed up to the entrance. "Hurry, everyone! Into the mountain!"

The four kids, with Max and Khan leading the way, charged between the raging fire monsters.

They ran into the opening.

They entered the world of the volcano.

Five

Smoke and Mirrors

They dashed through the dark entrance and found themselves in a vast cavern. The red glow from a lava pool lit the high walls around them.

"Phew! It smells burned in here," Neal whispered, creeping up behind Eric and Keeah. "Sort of like that brick oven pizza place back home."

"Without the good pizza smell," Eric added.

"Sparr is good at burning things," Khan said. "I hope to repay him for attacking my village."

Julie shivered. "You know, most people don't go inside a volcano. I hope we can get out."

"If we're careful, we will," Keeah said. "Now, first things first. Which way do we go?"

The cavern around them was dark and smoky. But it was empty. In the flickering red light, they saw a rough path dug out of the rock.

The path wound downward into the earth.

Eric knew where it led.

He wasn't sure *how* he knew, but he knew.

It led to the center of the volcano.

"We have to follow that path all the

way down," he said. "I have a feeling that's where Sparr keeps the Eye. Down there."

"How can you be sure?" Julie asked.

"Because the center is probably the scariest place anybody can think of," Keeah replied. "And Sparr would want to make it as hard as possible for anyone to find the Eye."

Max nodded. "And it *will* be harder, once he knows we are here."

Eric wondered how long it would take Sparr to find them poking around his secret hiding place. And what he would do when he did.

Khan sniffed. "Danger this way. Let's go on."

They all started down the winding path. It led below the level they had entered on, passing boiling pools that hissed and bubbled loudly.

They were being as quiet as they could be.

"The rock is getting hotter," Max said, crawling along the jagged walls of the path. "I wonder how we'll know when we reach the center."

"That's where they keep the lava," Neal said.

"Phew!" Julie sniffed. "What's that smell?"

Neal looked down. "My sneakers are on fire! Yikes! Now I know where my dream came from!" He stamped his sneakers until the fire went out. "Oh, man, that really hurt!"

"So do Ninns!" Eric hissed. "Quiet!"

The kids crept down to still another level.

The air was even hotter and smokier. It smelled worse. Keeah stopped. She held up her hand. "There's a cave up ahead," she whispered. "Something's moving. I saw a shadow —"

Suddenly, a figure stepped out of the cave.

"Guards, seize them!" a man said in a deep, snarly tone. The man was Lord Sparr!

"Whoa!" Neal gasped. "Let's get out of here!"

Everyone rushed back up the path, but Julie didn't move. She seemed frozen to the spot.

"Guards, seize them!" the sorcerer repeated in the same deep tone as before.

Eric dashed back to her. "Julie, come on! Sparr's the bad guy! Do I have to drag you out?"

"Wait a sec," Julie whispered.

"Wait?" Eric cried. "For big greasy Ninns to come clomping over and grab us? Come on!"

But Julie wouldn't budge. Seconds

passed and there were no clomping foot-steps. No greasy Ninn claws grabbing them.

Instead, Sparr turned stiffly and walked back into the cave. He appeared to touch the cave wall, but didn't quite touch it.

"See?" Julie murmured. "That's not him —"

"We'll be caught, you two!" Max cried, scampering up behind them with the others.

Julie laughed. "No, look. That isn't Sparr. I mean, it's not really Sparr. That is — I don't know what — special effects or something."

The figure strode forward again, not even blinking. Neal cringed as it stared icily at them.

"Guards, seize them!" Sparr repeated.

"Ha!" Julie said. "I don't think so, Sparr." Then she leaned forward and slapped the

sorcerer in the arm. Her hand went right through!

"Whoa!" Neal whispered.

"See what I mean?" Julie said.

Keeah nodded. "Maybe Sparr created a double to take his place because the jewel burned him. Maybe the real Sparr is hurt."

"Maybe it's done with mirrors," Eric said.

"Weird," said Neal, peering around the figure. "He's Sparr, but he's fake."

"Well, *they* aren't!" Max suddenly chirped.

The spider troll pointed at two giant red-faced Ninn soldiers. They came clomping down the passage right toward them.

"I thought I smelled something bad," Khan snorted, starting to run.

The Ninns grunted and hissed.

They pulled out big swords.

"GET THEM!" yelled the Ninns.

Six

Meeting the Witch

"Get the small ones!" the Ninns shouted. "And the purple Lumpy king, too!"

The kids shot down the passage like rockets.

They dived into the first cave they came to.

The two Ninns didn't see them. They charged away down the passage, thumping their big feet.

Eric breathed a sigh of relief. Then he

looked around. "Uh . . . who picked this cave?"

"You did!" Neal answered.

Instead of a hot, red cave, the space inside was tinted blue. A cool breeze blew through it.

And in the center was a large pool of the bluest water imaginable.

The surface of the water glistened and sparkled like glass.

"Whoa!" said Julie, peering around. "This is the place from my dream! This is what I saw!"

"Do you think it's regular water?" Eric asked.

"I don't see anything yucky," Neal said.

"I don't like it," Khan murmured.

Keeah stepped closer. "Let me test it out."

Keeah had told the kids she had powers. But they weren't exactly sure what she could do.

"Careful," said Eric. "This is Kano, don't forget. Sparr's home base."

Keeah reached for the water.

Suddenly, something with scaly skin slithered toward her from the far side of the pool.

"Watch out!" Julie cried. "A sea monster!"

Keeah jerked back from the edge of the pool.

A long, green, scaly tail broke the surface with a loud splash. It slapped down hard, and seconds later a head popped up out of the water.

It was the head of a woman!

"A mermaid!" Eric whispered.

Her skin was white, her lips were black. She had long, wet, green hair. Her shoul-

ders were dark and scaly. And her deep blue eyes narrowed as she looked from one child to the next.

"No," said Max. "Not a mermaid."

The woman spoke. "Who — are — you?"

Her voice was eerie and deep.

It seemed to come from every corner of the cave. Each word echoed off the stony walls.

Keeah glanced at her friends, then turned to the woman. "Uh . . . we . . . I am Keeah, Princess of Droon. And these are my friends."

The woman's eyes didn't move. "Friends from the Upper World. Sparr has spoken of you."

Julie shuddered. "What did he say about us? What does Lord Sparr know about us?"

But the woman didn't answer. She

turned to Keeah. "You have come for the Eye of Dawn."

Eric jumped. "How did you know that?"

"I am Demither," the woman said. "Some people say I am a witch. I know many things."

Her spiked tail flipped up suddenly. Water splashed on the cave walls and hissed.

"I've heard of you," Max twittered. "My master, Galen, has spoken of your evil deeds."

"Some choose to be evil," the witch said. "Some are forced to be evil." Demither clenched her teeth and dove under the water again.

"Something's weird," Eric said. "She looks like she's in pain or something."

"I am still afraid to trust her," Max said.

Splash! Demither rose again. "The Eye is in the Room of Fire!" She closed her eyes and groaned. "Cross the Bridge of Ice, and you will find it."

Keeah stepped to the edge. "If you know things, can you tell me how my mother died —"

"Your mother is alive!" the witch cried sharply. "Like me, she is cursed, in prison!"

Keeah gasped. "Prison! Here in the volcano?"

"Not here . . . everywhere!" the witch cried. "Find her. Help her — *as no one has helped me!*"

Seven

The Fierce Beast

The four kids all stared at Demither.

"So it's true!" Keeah exclaimed. "My mother is alive. I knew she was! I knew it!"

"Why are you helping us?" Eric asked the witch. "I thought you were a friend of Sparr."

"Friend!" the woman shrieked. She rose up ten feet in the air. Her scaly skin rippled and twisted as she curved up toward the cave's ceiling. "I — am — a — friend — of — no — one!"

"Wait," Keeah pleaded. "I need to know —"

But the witch's scaly body slithered back silently into the dark pool. The water hissed loudly as she passed under it.

Then the surface went still.

Demither was gone.

The kids looked at one another for a long time.

"It sounds like Sparr is forcing the witch to do bad stuff," Julie said finally. "Maybe he cursed your mother, Keeah."

"I don't like it," Max said. "Demither could be lying to us."

Keeah stared at the pool. "We need the Eye."

"Can the Eye do good things, too?" Eric asked her. "Can it, like, heal people and stuff?"

Keeah nodded. "Galen told me once that the jewel does what its owner wants it to."

"Cool," Neal mumbled. "I wish my dog did."

"But it is dangerous, too," said Khan. "Even Sparr was hurt by its power."

Eric turned to Keeah. "We'll get the Eye back for you. We'll do it, I promise. No matter —"

He never got a chance to finish.

Clomp, clomp! Heavy footsteps rushed toward the blue cave from the path outside.

"Hurry, or we'll be trapped!" Julie cried. She and Neal slipped out, with Max and Khan scrambling behind. But Eric and Keeah couldn't make it.

"Behind these rocks, quick!" Eric said to her.

They jumped behind a low pile of rocks near the cave entrance.

In marched ten Ninns. In between them crawled a strange, dark beast. It snarled and growled at the nervous-looking Ninns.

The beast stopped at the pool's edge.

"What is that thing?" Eric whispered to Keeah.

The princess shook her head. "I don't know."

The beast yowled sharply, as if it were hurt.

In the dim light, Eric could see that the creature had four thick, clawed legs and a long body.

Its skin was black and bumpy from its large head all the way to its long, spiked tail.

On the top of its head were rows of large, pointed ears, like bat's ears.

Eric's stomach turned just looking at the ugly thing. He swallowed hard. "It's some kind of weird, horrible monster."

"Is this Sparr's secret weapon?" Keeah asked.

Eric struggled to keep his food down. "Maybe *this* is his secret. The one in my dream. The secret Sparr thought I knew. He keeps a monster for a pet."

Suddenly, the creature charged forward and leaped to the pool. It began to slurp loudly.

"Let's get out of here," Keeah whispered. "That thing could turn on us."

Eric began to tremble. "Wait . . ."

They watched the beast drink and drink.

Eric turned to Keeah. She looked at him.

Then they looked back at the creature.

Their eyes went wide with amazement.

"No!" Eric gasped softly. "It . . . can't . . . be!"

Eight

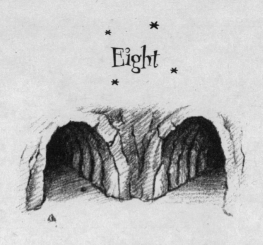

Sparr's Secret?

As the beast slurped from the pool, it began to change. Its dark, spiky hide shrank away. One by one, the sharp claws shriveled. Two became hands, two became feet.

Pale, smooth skin formed over the head.

The creature's arms and legs began to grow longer.

Suddenly, the thing stood upright. Like a man.

All that remained of the monster were two pointed fins growing behind the ears.

Eric caught his breath. "Holy crow!"

The man threw his powerful arms into the air.

Deep, frightening laughter filled the cavern.

The man was Lord Sparr!

Without taking a breath, Eric and Keeah crept from the cave and ran quickly down the path.

"I can't believe it!" Eric whispered. "Sparr's a monster! A creature! A creepy beast thing!"

Keeah shivered. "Remember what Khan told us? The Eye of Dawn burned Sparr. Maybe it did worse things. Maybe it made him like this."

"Yeah, and he drinks from the pool to make himself human again," Eric said. "Because if he doesn't, he changes back into this — *thing*! Maybe *that's* his secret! Just like in my dream!"

Julie, Neal, Max, and Khan ran up to them.

"Are you guys okay?" Julie asked.

"You'll never believe what we saw!" Keeah said. "There was a —"

But Keeah didn't get to finish.

Lord Sparr stepped out of the shadows.

"Ninns! I have found them!" the sorcerer said in a snarly tone. His eyes flashed at the kids.

Neal laughed suddenly. "Oh, look. Mr. Special Effects is back! Guys, let me handle this."

"Neal, no!" Eric began.

Neal stuck his hands behind his ears and wiggled them as if they were fins. "Fake Sparr! Fake Sparr!"

Then he marched up to the sorcerer, stood right in front of him, and made a fist. "Now, I'm going to punch right through your bogus self!"

"Neal, don't," Keeah said. "It's really —"

Smack! Neal's fist stopped at Sparr's arm.

Neal frowned. "It's supposed to go through." He turned to Julie. "It went through for you."

"Neal . . ." Julie said.

Neal punched Sparr again. *Smack!*

"Oh, now I get it." Neal said quietly. "Ouch."

"NINNS!" the sorcerer shouted at the top of his lungs. The passageway filled with red-faced warriors.

The kids were surrounded.

Keeah's eyes burned with anger. "We know your secret, Sparr. You're a monster!"

"A creepy one!" said Eric. "Much creepier than you are now. Which is pretty creepy!"

The sorcerer's lips curled into an evil snarl. His eyes darkened. His purple fins began to curl.

"Now you can never leave!" he said. His muscled hand clamped down on Neal's shoulder.

Neal screeched. "It's because I did hands behind the ears, isn't it? You didn't like that."

"You leave my best friend alone!" Eric yelled. He jumped as hard as he could on Sparr's feet.

"Ahhh!" The sorcerer released Neal.

"I sniff an escape this way!" Khan yelled.

The six friends shot away down the narrow passage. They were still going deeper into the volcano.

Sparr leaped into the air after them. He

flew like a bullet, swooping through the tunnels, screaming strange words. *"Selam! Ala! Kwitt!"*

"Same to you!" Julie shouted back.

Eric and Keeah were in the lead, threading through the curving passages.

Suddenly, the passage split before them. Two tunnels lay ahead. Both were dark.

"Left! Left!" Keeah cried.

Eric flashed a look at his hands. He couldn't decide. *Left? Left!* He kept running toward the passages. He ran faster.

"Hurry!" the princess shouted.

Right? Left! Huh? This is so dumb! With all the smoke and darkness, he couldn't even see!

Eric picked one dark passage, running into it as fast as he could. He wanted to get as far as possible from Sparr. He'd discovered his secret.

But now sounds were swirling all around him.

Hissing and bubbling. Clomping and stomping. Eric stole a quick look backward.

It was dark. He couldn't see Keeah anywhere.

He slowed to a stop. "Guys? Are you back there in the dark? Oh, man, please answer!"

No answer.

Eric swallowed hard. "Sp-Sparr? Please *don't* answer. . . ."

No answer. Eric was alone in the dark.

He couldn't tell front from back. Right from left. Up from down.

"Where am I?" he breathed.

Splurt — ssss! A sudden fiery splash of lava burst from the volcano floor. It flashed against the walls of a vast cavern. Smoking red lava bubbled and hissed away into the far distance.

"It's a lake," Eric gasped. "A lake of lava!"

He knew right away where he was.

He had found it.

The Room of Fire.

Nine

Fountain of Danger

Splursh! The fiery column spurted again. It was coming from a strange fountain on a small island in the center of the lake. The fountain was formed of craggy, hardened lava.

Then Eric noticed something else.

Near the top of the fountain, and sheltered from its spray, was a dome of glass.

Inside the dome was a strange black object.

An armored glove with a red jewel on it.

"The Eye of Dawn!" Eric said to himself. "Just like Demither said."

But the fountain lay in the center of a lake of burning, bubbling lava. He would burn to a crisp if he took one step into it. Then he remembered what else Demither had told them.

Cross the Bridge of Ice.

Eric circled the shore of the lava lake. Something about the lava's surface seemed strange.

Some parts of it didn't move the same as in other places. He bent down at one spot and gazed across the top of the lava.

A narrow strip of something clear lay just above the bubbling surface. It looked like a strip of glass, stretching from the shore to the island.

"The Bridge of Ice!" he said.

Carefully, he stepped onto the bridge. It

held him. He took another step. He felt as if he were walking a tightrope. But he kept going.

Soon he was halfway across. Halfway to the island. To the stone fountain itself. To the Eye!

Splursh! The fountain exploded with a giant spurt of molten rock. Fiery spray shot to the ceiling and showered back down to the giant lake.

Tssss! The rocks hit the surface all around him.

But Eric kept going. He couldn't turn back. Not until he got what they had come for.

"We have to stop Lord Sparr," he said firmly.

Splursh! The fountain went off again. *Tssss!*

Eric timed it to see how long he had until the next eruption. "One Mississippi, two Mississippi, three Mississippi, four Mississippi —"

Splursh! Tssss!

"Four seconds," Eric told himself. He took a deep breath, ran to the end of the bridge, and sprang off. He landed at the base of the fountain.

One Mississippi . . .

In two quick moves, he was up to the top of the fountain. Using a rock, he broke the glass dome and grabbed the black glove.

Two Mississippi . . .

He jumped down to the base of the fountain. But the rocks were covered with a thin layer of ashes. His sneakers slid on them. He tried to steady himself. He hit the ground. "Ooof!"

Three Mississippi . . .

Plonk! The glove fell from his hand.

"No!" Eric yelled out. He reached out

wildly for the glove. His fingers fumbled for it.

Four Mississippi!

SPLURSH! Molten rocks exploded up from the fountain to the ceiling. Then they began to fall.

Eric grabbed the glove and pulled it on.

The fiery rocks seemed to aim right for him.

"Nooooo!" he screamed, throwing his arms up to shield himself from the burning rocks.

Suddenly, the Eye of Dawn began to glow.

Blam! Blam! Blam! Flashes of red light shot from the glove's fingertips. The molten rocks blasted apart in midair. One after another, the chunks of molten stone exploded to nothing.

Eric's hand was going crazy. He couldn't

control the Eye. It blew up everything in sight.

Blam! Blam! The fountain itself shattered into a thousand pieces.

"Whoa!" Eric cried. "Glove, stop! Eye, stop!"

But the Red Eye of Dawn wouldn't stop.

Eric struggled to his feet and rushed onto the bridge of ice. Then the Eye forced his hand around and blasted the bridge! *Ka-whoom!*

He dived to shore as the bridge exploded into a million little pieces.

The walls of the cavern were starting to quake. The volcano floor was rumbling. The lava lake swelled. Waves churned and splashed.

"Uh-oh!" he gasped, scrambling up. "I think I started something! And it's not good!"

"Eric!" someone shouted.

He turned. It was Keeah, running into the cavern. Behind her were Julie, Neal, Khan, and Max.

"I've got the Eye!" Eric shouted to them. "But I can't control it too well!"

Blam! Blam! The glove blasted the black walls two feet away from his friends' heads.

"We get the idea!" Keeah shouted. She ran over and grabbed Eric's hand. Suddenly, the glove became steady. It seemed as if a power moved through Keeah's hand to his own.

"Good work, Eric!" Julie cried. "You did it!"

"Save the praise for later," Max chirped. "Here comes Lord Sparr!"

"Grab Eric's hand," shouted Keeah.

Neal, Julie, Max, and Khan put their hands over Keeah's and Eric's. Keeah focused the glove toward the far wall.

KA-WHOOM! The Eye blew a hole

clear through the volcano wall! Daylight shone through the hole.

The force of the Eye pulled the kids from the ground. It shot them through the rocky passage like a rocket.

"I will follow you — forever!" cried Lord Sparr, charging in as the black walls of his volcano home began to crumble.

Ten

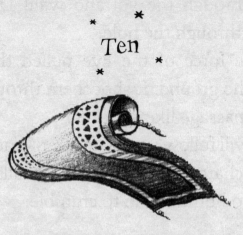

The Door Home

"Whoaaa!" Eric shrieked as the six friends barreled out through the volcano at top speed.

Then — *splat-at-at-at-at-at!*

They hit a wall. Luckily, it was a soft wall. It was a wall made of sand. It was a sand dune.

"We're outside!" Julie yelled. "Yahoo!"

"There they are!" cried a voice. Galen rode up quickly. Behind him, the Lumpies had just finished tying the fire monsters in a giant knot.

"Yes!" Max chittered. "My master is safe!"

"We have the Eye!" Keeah called out.

Galen's eyes lit up. "My friends, you have done well!" Carefully, he took the glove from Eric. He closed his hands around it and put it safely in a golden box in Leep's saddlebag.

"We must leave Kano at once," the wizard said. "Keeah, your father's ship is waiting at the coast. The stairs to the Upper World have appeared there, too. Max, come. Hurry, everyone. Hurry!"

Max jumped up on Leep's head. "The way out is in the West! The old riddle says, it cannot be seen where it is!"

Eric sighed. "Another riddle? Can't anything in Droon be easy?"

"This will make it easier," Khan said. *Flump!* He tossed something heavy on the sand. "A carpet from Pasha."

"A flying carpet!" Julie exclaimed.

"The perfect escape vehicle!" Neal added.

"Better hurry," Khan cried, sniffing the smoky air. "Groggles — lots of them. Coming fast!"

Out of the smoke came dozens of Ninns on their ugly flying lizards called groggles. Huge flapping wings darkened the dark air even more.

Kaww! Kaww! the groggles cried.

"Let's see how fast this baby can go," Julie said. "Everybody on Pasha's rug! Now — *fly!*"

Whoosh! The carpet lifted into the wind and soared up over the volcano. As Galen, Max, Khan, and the Lumpies galloped away, Julie tugged at a corner, and the carpet shot out across the dunes.

But the flying groggles were fast, too. They chased the kids for mile after mile, getting closer and closer.

Eric scanned the desert ahead. In the middle of the dunes was a single rock. It was tall and wide and stuck straight up from the desert floor.

"Watch out for that rock," Keeah said.

"Yeah," Neal added, "we definitely don't want to crash into that!"

"Right . . ." Eric began. Then he shook his head. "No, head *for* it! The riddle says that the way out cannot be seen where it is. The way out is *through the rock*!"

"Are you sure?" Julie asked.

"Trust me!" Eric said.

Kaww! The groggles were right behind them.

The rock was right ahead of them.

"It sure looks solid!" Neal cried, shutting his eyes and clutching the carpet tight. "I hope this works!"

Around the rock was open air, stretching into the distance. Still, the kids dove for the rock.

They went . . . *into* the rock.

Whoosh! At the moment the carpet hit the rock, the rock became an opening. At the same moment, the air around it became solid rock.

"Agh!" the Ninns cried. Their groggles lurched away, nearly smashing into the wall of rock.

"Hooray!" Eric held on tight as they swept into a world of trees and rivers and meadows.

The air was clear and fresh. It smelled sweet.

"We're out of Kano!" Keeah said, pointing to the distance. "And heading for the coast."

Minutes later, they landed on a sandy shore. A blue ocean rolled gently to the distant horizon.

And the stairs back to Eric's house glittered nearby, hovering inches above the beach.

A grand wooden ship was floating in a peaceful bay. It had white-and-pink sails and a blue smokestack. The ship's sides swept back from a sharp point in front to twin wings in the rear.

"Today, we won," Keeah said. "We learned that Sparr is some kind of — creature."

"He turns back into it sometimes," Eric said. "And he needs to drink from the witch's pool."

"It's weird," said Neal. "How all our dreams sort of came true. . . ."

Eric shook his head. "I guess there are still lots of secrets about Droon we don't know."

"Like the whole story about the witch, Demither," Julie added. "She was strange. Kind of sad, too."

Keeah breathed in, smiling. "She said my mother is alive, under a curse somewhere. If she is, I'm going to find her and set her free."

"We'll help you," Eric said. "We'll be back as soon as we can."

"Definitely," Neal said. "Count me in!"

"Count us all in," Julie added.

As the kids made their way to the magic stairs, a pilka whinnied behind them. *Hrrr!*

They turned to see Galen, Max, and Khan riding down the beach toward them. They waved.

"You're safe now," Eric said to Keeah. "I guess we'd better go before the stairs fade."

"The magic of Droon goes with you," Keeah said, waving. "It will tell you when to return!"

The three friends raced up the magic stairs. At the top, Eric turned to look back at Droon.

"I hope the adventure never ends," Julie said.

Eric smiled. "Something tells me it never will. There are too many secrets we don't know yet."

"And too much work for us to do," Neal said.

Julie laughed. "There's plenty of work for us up here, too. In our normal lives. We said we'd clean up the basement, remember?"

They all stepped up into the room at the top of the stairs. Neal flicked the light switch.

Click! The land of Droon vanished. In its place was the plain old cement floor.

"We're home," Eric murmured. He put his hand on the doorknob and opened the door.

The three friends went out into the basement.

The messy, messy basement.

They got to work.

The Mysterious Island

by Tony Abbott
Illustrated by David Merrell

To all children
who explore and dream
and imagine

One

The Storm

Keee-kkkk! Lightning crackled and flashed outside the windows of Eric Hinkle's basement.

But he and his friend Julie could only look at the soccer ball in the corner.

Boooom! The thunder two seconds later told them the storm was only a couple of miles away.

"Neal is going to freak out when he

sees," said Eric. Neal was Eric and Julie's friend.

Julie stared over his shoulder. "I'm freaking out already," she said. "Let's call him. His eyes will bug out. He's got to see this — now."

The two friends ran up the basement stairs to the kitchen. Eric picked up the telephone and punched in Neal's number. Another flash of lightning made the phone crackle in his ear.

"Hello, Neal?" Eric said when his friend answered. "You've got to come over right away."

"Are you kidding? There's going to be a humongous storm in five minutes," Neal replied. "Besides, I'm getting ready to eat. It's lunchtime."

"It's always lunchtime for you," Eric said. "Forget food, Neal. This is important."

Neal sighed. "It'd better be, for me to pass up one of my mom's tuna fish sandwiches. I'm coming."

After Neal hung up, Eric and Julie glanced out the window. The sky was getting very dark.

Eric began to smile. "Good day to hang out in my basement."

"You mean, hang out in Droon," Julie added.

Eric chuckled. "Of course that's what I mean."

In Eric's basement there was an entrance to another world.

A world that Eric, Julie, and Neal kept secret. The mysterious and magical world of Droon.

Droon was a place where a good wizard called Galen Longbeard and a young princess named Keeah battled a very evil sorcerer by the name of Lord Sparr.

Droon had all kinds of strange creatures, too. Galen's assistant, Max, was a spider troll, half spider, half troll. He could climb up anything and spin sticky webs with his eight long legs.

And then there were the Ninns. They were Lord Sparr's nasty, red-faced warriors who flew around on big lizards known as groggles.

And a witch named Demither. And —

Boom-ba-boom! The sky flashed outside, and thunder boomed just as the back door opened.

"Yikes!" Neal charged into the kitchen. "I think that storm followed me!"

Eric opened the basement door. "No time for talk. Everybody downstairs."

The moment they got to the bottom of the stairs — *kkkkk!* — the basement flashed white, and — *ba-boom!* — the walls rumbled, and — *splish!* — rain splashed hard against the house.

"*Hello*, storm," Julie said.

"All right," said Neal, stepping into the basement. "What is more important than tuna fish sandwiches?"

"That." Eric pointed to a corner of the basement. The soccer ball — Julie's soccer ball — was sitting on the workbench.

Actually, it was sitting *above* the workbench.

It was floating in the air.

"Whoa!" Neal gasped. "I repeat — whoa!"

"Not only that," Eric said. "You remember the first time we went to Droon and the soccer ball came with us and then it did that magical thing when we came back? Well, Julie and I were looking at it before, and —"

"Shhh!" Julie whispered. "It's doing it again!"

By the glow of the ceiling light they watched the ball begin to change.

The black and white patches moved slowly across the surface of the ball. The patches became the shapes of countries. And the ball itself became a globe of another world.

The world of Droon.

"It means we need to go," Julie said, looking at her two friends. "What else could it mean?"

"Last time, our dreams told us to go to Droon," Eric said. "But this is different. I think it's a sign from Keeah."

Neal took a deep breath. "What if something bad is happening? What if Lord Sparr is, like, attacking Keeah? Or Galen?"

Kaaa-kkkk! The room flashed white.

The lightbulb in the ceiling flickered and dimmed.

"There's only one way to find out," Eric said.

Doom-da-doom! Thunder exploded overhead.

"Hurry before the power goes," Julie added.

Eric felt his heart race as they went to the closet under the steps. Just like the other times, he pulled the door open and turned on the light.

They entered the small room.

Where are we going this time? Eric wondered.

So far, the stairs had never taken them to the same place twice. And the stairway always faded and reappeared in a new part of Droon.

That was just one of the secrets of Droon.

Julie shut the door behind them. Neal flicked off the light. The room was dark for an instant.

Then it wasn't.

Whoosh! The floor vanished, and a long flight of colored stairs shimmered into place.

"I love that!" said Eric.

A sudden, cold wind blew into their faces.

"Whoa!" Julie said. "Hold onto the railing."

"Hold your nose!" Neal said. "I smell fish!"

"Seawater!" said Eric. "The stairs are over an ocean or something. Maybe we should go back."

But even as he said that, it was too late.

Shloosh! — a huge wave of icy water splashed across the stairs.

Eric's feet slipped out from under him.

"Help!" He clutched for the railing. He missed.

"Eric!" Julie grasped his hand, but another wave followed the first. Eric slid off the stairs, pulling Julie with him. She grabbed for something to hold on to.

"That's my foot!" Neal yelled.

Neal slipped down, too.

Splish! Splash! Sploosh!

The three friends hit the water hard.

"Neal! Julie!" Eric cried.

Tall waves leaped and crashed around him.

"I'm here!" Julie shouted, gulping for air.

"Something's coming!" Neal yelled.

A dark shape plowed across the waves. It was the bow of a giant ship.

"Watch out for us!" Eric shouted.

But the ship charged toward them, faster and faster.

Two

Wings Over Water

Suddenly the ship slowed.

"Down sail!" boomed a deep voice above them. "Circle around! Drop a rope!"

Splash! A thick rope slapped the surface of the water. Eric, Neal, and Julie grabbed hold of the rope and climbed up.

The ship was huge, with red-and-yellow sails and blue wings that swept to the back.

As he climbed, Eric read the golden letters on the ship's side.

"The *Jaffa Wind*. Jaffa City is where Princess Keeah lives. This must be her boat!"

A strong hand reached down and helped them aboard.

"Our friends from the Upper World!" said a man in a long blue robe, smiling at them. It was Galen Longbeard, first wizard of Droon.

"You have come to us again," he said. "And again we can offer you nothing but danger."

"We had to come," Julie said. "The soccer ball turned into a globe of Droon. Did Keeah do that?"

"Eric! Julie! Neal!" cried Princess Keeah, running over. "You got my message. The magic must be working. I'm so happy to see you." She gave them all big hugs even though they were soaking wet.

"How can anyone be happy with *that* thing on board?" snapped Max. The spider troll's orange hair stood on end as he pointed to a small gold chest on the deck.

"Whoa," Neal said. "The Red Eye of Dawn is in there!"

The Red Eye of Dawn was a jewel of amazing power. Neal, Eric, and Julie had helped Keeah steal it from Lord Sparr's volcano palace.

"We're going to hide it in Jaffa City," said Keeah. "We can use your help. Then my father and I are going to search for my mother."

"You can count on us," said Eric.

A strange witch named Demither had told them that Keeah's mother was alive. But, like Demither herself, Queen Relna was under a curse.

Galen nodded. "But Sparr will do whatever he can to stop us. It is his angry heart that makes the Red Eye so dangerous. Come, we must hurry."

Ker-splash! Icy waves crashed against the sides of the ship as it gathered speed once again.

"With two wizards aboard we should be safe," Eric said, looking at Galen and Keeah.

"One and a half," Keeah said. "I've been practicing spells. But so far all I do is break things. Like this morning —"

Kkkk! A sudden bolt of lightning lit up the sky.

A dark swarm streaked across the clouds.

"Uh-oh," Neal said. "Unless I'm crazy, Lord Sparr has found us! And he's not alone!"

"Groggles!" Eric hissed. "Hundreds of them."

The sea bubbled suddenly like a cauldron. Waves splashed up higher and higher. Rain fell on the deck in big icy drops.

"Looks like he is bringing foul weather with him, too!" Max snapped. "Prepare for battle!"

The swarm of groggles flew low over the ship.

One of the flying lizards swooped down and landed on the deck. On its back was the evil sorcerer himself — Lord Sparr.

"Get away from my ship!" Keeah cried.

The sorcerer snarled as he slid off the groggle. His bald head gleamed. The fins behind his ears turned from purple to black. In his hand he held a long staff.

"Beware, Sparr," Galen boomed. "You are outnumbered."

"Right," said Julie. "And we're keeping the jewel! So you can forget about taking it."

Sparr's eyes flashed at the children.

"Ah, the magic stairs brought you again? When the Eye is mine, I'll climb those stairs to the Upper World!"

Eric shivered. *Sparr? In my world? My house?*

Without warning Sparr thrust his magic staff at the golden chest.

Ka-blam! The box blasted open, and a black armored glove tumbled across the deck. Fitted into the glove was the Red Eye of Dawn.

"You wicked creature!" Galen cried. "I will not let you have it!" He threw a sizzling bolt of blue light at Sparr. *Ka-koom!*

But Sparr's staff sucked up the light and threw it back at Galen.

Then the sorcerer grabbed the glove and slipped it on. Bright red light shot from its fingertips. "Your powers are weak, Galen. Now — Red Eye of Dawn, show me your power! Create for me a sea of fire!"

Ka-whoosh! A wall of fiery water rose up suddenly. The kids tumbled to the deck.

"Keeah!" yelled Eric. "Do a spell!"

"Break something big!" Julie cried. "Real big!"

Keeah struggled to her feet and aimed her fingers at the giant mast. *"Bembo — switt!"*

Suddenly — *crack!* — the towering mast split in half and fell toward Sparr.

Whoomf! Sparr was slammed back against the main cabin. The black glove was thrown from his hand.

"Yes!" Keeah shouted.

Galen leaped across the deck. Grabbing the glove, he flung it into the golden chest and held the lid down tight.

Sparr's face wrinkled in horror. "That power belongs to *me*! Rise, O Demither!"

"Demither?" Eric cried. "The witch?"

The waves thundered below. A huge

green serpent burst through the water. It had sawlike teeth, two powerful claws, and a long, spiky tail.

"The witch is a sea monster now!" Neal cried.

The serpent twisted her mighty tail around the ship and pulled tight.

Crack! The ship's planks began to break.

"The hull is splitting!" Max yelled out.

"And you will all drown!" Sparr howled, jumping back onto his groggle.

Keeah threw a thick rope to Julie. "Everyone hold tight!" Neal lunged and grabbed the rope.

"Eric," Keeah yelled. "Take the rope!"

"I can't reach it!" he cried.

The serpent witch lifted the ship high above the waves. She held it there for a moment and then threw it back down into the water.

Krrrrunch! The wooden hull shattered into shreds. And the *Jaffa Wind,* with everyone aboard, broke in two.

The ship sank instantly beneath the waves.

Three

Shipwrecked!

Eric's world went black and bubbly.

No! he thought. *This can't happen! I can't sink!*

He clawed at the icy water, trying to reach the surface. Then the waves opened above him. Eric lifted his head out of the water. His fingers felt something soft.

Was it . . . sand?

Yes! It was sand. Eric scrambled up

onto it. He sucked in a deep, deep breath. He opened his eyes.

He was on land, on a beach. He was alive.

"Julie! Neal! Keeah!" he called out.

No answer.

Eric looked to his left. All he saw was the beach stretching away until it curved out of sight. He looked to the right and saw the waves splashing against piles of rocks. Ahead of him was a thick jungle full of odd-shaped bushes and tall trees.

A dark haze hung over the treetops. The whole island was covered in fog.

"What *is* this place?" he said to himself.

Splursh! Another wave crashed against the nearby rocks. Something tumbled onto the sand.

Eric ran to the rocks. The waves had washed up some broken boards and a torn piece of cloth. They were from Keeah's ship.

Next to them, half covered by sand, was . . .

"The golden chest!" Eric gasped.

With the Eye, he knew, anything was possible. Maybe he could use it to find his friends. Maybe even to fight Sparr.

But where was Galen?

Where was everybody?

Carefully, Eric lifted the chest from the sand. He opened it. But instead of finding the black glove with the red stone, flames jumped up at him.

"Ahh!" Eric cried, nearly dropping the chest.

Suddenly the fire changed. Before his eyes the fire became hundreds of snaky creatures, slithering over one another.

They gleamed red, then silver, then red again. Sometimes they looked like flames. Sometimes they looked like rippling ropes of water.

"Don't eat us-s-s!" the creatures pleaded.

Eric set the chest carefully on the sand. "I'm not going to eat you. But . . . who are you?"

Many tiny silver heads twisted toward him.

"We are s-s-silfs. We have lived-d-d for centuries in the s-s-seas of Droon. Demither-r-r is our queen."

The sound the creatures made was more like singing than speaking. Their bubbly voices sounded as though they were talking underwater.

"Demither sank our ship," said Eric.

"Sparr has put a curse on her-r-r," one silf sang. "She must do things she doesn't want to-o-o. The Eye will give Sparr even more power-r-r."

Eric shook his head. "The Eye was lost at sea."

"No!" the silfs sang. "It is on this-s-s is-

land. This is one of Demither's-s-s many islands."

"The Eye is here?" Eric asked. "Where? I have to find it. I have to help Princess Keeah get it to Jaffa City."

Thwomp! Thwomp! A deep thumping sound came from down the beach.

"Hide," the silfs cried. "Ninns-s-s are coming!"

"Wait," Eric called out. "Help me find my friends. And tell me where the Eye is!"

"If we can-n-n help you, we will-l-l. . . ."

The creatures turned fiery red, then silver. Then they slid over the sand and away into the waves.

Thwomp! Dozens of heavy, red-faced warriors came marching slowly up the beach.

"Ninns!" Eric gasped. "I am out of here!"

Eric ran quickly into the thick jungle.

Strange and wild plants slapped him in the face as he raced. Slippery yellow vines coiled down from above and dangled in the paths.

The Ninns' thumping got louder.

Eric ran faster.

Suddenly the ground turned soft beneath him.

"Huh?" He stumbled and fell.

Fwit! A sticky web surrounded Eric like a sack. It pulled tight around him.

He couldn't get out. Then the sack — with Eric inside — flew into the air. It went up high into the yellow trees.

"Please, no!" he yelled. "Help, I'm trapped!"

He couldn't escape.

Thwomp! Thwomp! The Ninns marched closer.

✷ Four ✷

Trapped . . . with Friends

Eric pushed and pulled as hard as he could to break out of the sack. The more he struggled, the more he got tangled in its sticky web.

"Get me out of here!" he cried.

And still he was pulled higher into the yellow trees.

"Stop making so much noise!" hissed a voice from above. "Do you want the whole Ninn army to hear you?"

Eric stopped going up. The sack swung back and forth from a high branch. A branch someone was sitting on. "Kee-ah?"

The princess smiled at him. "And Max, too."

"Of course!" Max chirped from the branch above. "Who do you think spun this little trap?"

"Boy, am I glad to see you," Eric said. He told them quickly about the silfs.

"I've heard of the silfs, but I've never seen them," said Keeah.

"They told me the Red Eye is on this island," said Eric. "We need to find it."

Thwomp! Thwomp! The Ninns crossed the beach and marched into the jungle right below them.

"Galen is on the island, too," Keeah said. "But, look —"

In the middle of the troop of Ninns was

the wizard, wrapped from head to foot in thick chains.

Galen was their prisoner!

"My poor master!" Max whimpered.

One of the red-faced warriors below held up his six-fingered claw. "Sparr said wait here."

"He wants the old man alive," said another.

"For now, at least!" a third said, laughing.

The laughter reminded Eric of gargling.

A cold wind blew through the trees.

Keeah gritted her teeth as she looked up. "Sparr is coming!" she snarled.

A groggle landed on the ground. Lord Sparr slid off its back. He pointed his magic staff at Galen. "You know where the Eye is. Tell me."

Galen stared at Sparr. "Never. You may

put me in chains. But the children are brave and clever. They will trick you."

"Demither's island has many dangers," Sparr said. "Anything can happen. In the end, the Eye will be mine."

Galen struggled against his chains. "The children will find the jewel."

A thin smile broke across Sparr's lips. "And they will give it to me, *if* they want you to live. If I find it, it's mine. If they find it, it's also mine. Either way, I win."

Galen shook his head sadly. "You were not always so evil, Sparr!"

The sorcerer turned to the Ninns. "Take the wizard to the white cliff. Wait for my orders."

"At once, Lord Sparr," the head Ninn said.

Then Sparr waved his hand and spoke a strange word. The whole troop of Ninns, along with Galen, vanished.

"Oh, no!" Max whispered. "How will we find my master now?"

Keeah put her finger to her lips as Sparr began to laugh.

"Galen's 'brave' children will never get off this island alive!"

Sparr jumped onto his groggle, kicked once, and flew away. As he did, the thick, dark mist all over the island seemed to grow thicker and darker.

"Never get off this island alive?" Eric snarled. "Ha!"

Then he gulped. "We will, won't we?"

"Yes, if we find my master," Max said. "And when we do, I will kick Sparr with each of my eight legs!" Then he quickly spun a strong rope of spider silk, and they all slid to the ground.

Eric waved at the thick haze. "Now where do we go?"

"Yikes!" a voice screamed suddenly.

"Help us!" another voice screamed.

"I think that just answered my question!" Eric said.

"It's Julie and Neal!" Keeah said. "They're in the jungle. Let's go!"

They crashed through the thick trees as fast as they could. The long vines whipped against their faces. The bushes scratched them.

Suddenly they froze.

Julie and Neal were standing on a rock in the middle of a clearing.

Surrounding them were six nasty, icky, enormous —

"Bugs!" cried Max.

Five

Attack of the Icky Bugs

Sssss! The giant bugs hissed angrily at Neal. Their thick, pointed tongues lashed up at him.

"If one of those things licks me, I'm going to lose the lunch I never ate!" Neal shouted.

The bugs were hairy beetles about four feet long. Their hard brown shells gleamed like armor.

"Gross!" said Eric, ducking behind a tree.

"Eew!" said Keeah, jumping down beside him.

The bugs flicked their fuzzy legs at Neal and Julie. Their feelers twitched, and their tongues stuck out angrily.

"All I did was look at a rock," Neal said.

"It was an egg!" Julie shouted, pointing to a nearby pile of round pink eggs. "One of *their* eggs! And you didn't look, you touched!"

Neal shrugged. "So how do you say 'I'm sorry' in bug language?"

"If they even *have* a language," Max said. "The horrible creatures!"

Sssss! The bugs hissed and edged even closer.

Keeah turned to Eric and Max. "I'm going to try a spell. If it works, it will scare

the bugs for a few seconds. Then you two can help Neal and Julie escape."

"We will do it!" Max promised.

Keeah crossed her fingers. "Right, *if* I concentrate on something simple . . ."

Eric peered around the tree. "On the count of three, you guys run, okay?"

"How about on the count of one?" Neal asked.

"Very funny," Eric said. "One . . ."

Keeah jumped up. She pointed her hands at the bugs.

"Two . . ." said Eric.

Keeah narrowed her eyes. *"Tomba — snooka — jeeba —"*

". . . three!" Eric shouted.

"Three!" said Keeah. "No, wait! I mean *floo*!"

Too late. Neal and Julie were already leaping off the rock when — *ka-bam!* — a bolt of bright green light shot from Keeah's hands.

The air filled with smoke. The bugs shrieked — *eeee!* — and disappeared into the jungle.

Julie leaped over to the princess. "Keeah, you did it! Your incredible spell worked!"

Keeah stared at her hands. "I guess so. . . ."

Eric tried to wave away the smoke. "Where's Neal?"

"Here I am!" he yelled from behind them.

Julie and Eric turned around. Neal wasn't standing there. The only thing there was the pile of bug eggs.

"I hear him," Julie said, "but I don't see him."

"Hey, I'm right here!" Neal shouted again.

The pile of pink eggs moved. Out from underneath the pile popped a brown bug twice the size of a football. It had a hard, shiny shell, six thin legs with fuzz on them, three orange eyes, and two feelers sticking out from its head.

It was like all the other bugs only smaller.

A baby bug.

Eric staggered back. "Neal, is that . . . *you*?"

The brown bug scuttled across the pile of eggs and looked up at them. "Boy," the bug said in Neal's voice, "Keeah's spell made you sort of big, didn't it?"

Eric gulped. "The spell went wrong, all right," he began. "But . . . well, um, Neal, it's like, I mean —"

"You're a bug!" Julie shouted. "An icky icky bug!"

"The spider part of me resents that!" said Max.

"Oh, what have I done?" Keeah said. "Neal, I am *so* sorry!"

Neal rubbed his front legs together. Then he saw them and jumped. "Oh, man! This is not good. Change me back, Keeah. Change me back now!"

The princess stared at her fingertips and then back at Neal.

"You didn't answer right away!" Neal said. "You're supposed to say, 'Sure, Neal!' and do your zapping thing, and I'm *me* again." Neal closed his three eyes. "I'm ready. Go."

Keeah's own eyes welled up with tears. "I'm afraid to try."

Neal's fuzzy legs began to quiver, and his feelers twitched. "It's all a dream. It's all a dream. It's all a — hey, what's that?"

Suddenly he flicked his tongue at Julie's head.

"Eeeeeew!" she gasped, jerking backward.

"Sorry. There was a fly near you," Neal said. "At least it looked like a fly. It was yellow with bright green wings. Anyway, I missed it."

"What you saw was a Droonian seafly," Max said.

Suddenly Neal rubbed his legs together, making a strange, high-pitched sound.

Eric made a face. "Stop being such a bug."

"Shhh!" Neal hissed. He tilted his head and went still. "Say that again, please."

Eric blinked. "I said, stop being such a —"

"Not you!" Neal snapped. "The fly!"

Neal's big eyes flickered as the green-winged insect buzzed in a quick circle around his head. He kept nodding.

Eric turned to Keeah. "I don't hear anything."

Julie bit her lip. Then she brightened. "Maybe now that Neal is part insect he can understand the seafly language."

"I'm too much of a troll to understand it myself," said Max.

Soon there was a whole swarm of seaflies buzzing over them.

Neal scratched his head with his front legs. "They tell me that the groggles are nesting up there somewhere." He pointed up.

"Where there are groggles, there are Ninns," said Keeah. "And where there are Ninns —"

"There is my master, Galen!" Max chirped.

Julie looked up into the fog. "But

what's up there? It's too foggy to see any-thing."

Neal nodded and twitched his feelers a few times. The flies swarmed together in a dense, bright green lump. They began to buzz in ever-widening circles. Faster and faster they flew, around and around over the kids' heads, stirring up the air.

And as they did, the breeze they made began to clear away the dark fog.

Keeah looked up. "Oh, my gosh!" she gasped. "A mountain!"

Six

Groggle Mountain

Julie stared up. "You mean that was there the whole time?"

The mountain was steep and craggy. Its distant peak went through the clouds high above the island.

"It's awesome," said Eric. "I bet the white cliff is at the top. That's where Galen is being held prisoner."

"If Galen is at the top," Keeah said, "then to the top we're going! Max?"

"At once, my princess!" the spider troll replied. Then he began to spin his legs so quickly they seemed to blur. Moments later, he held a long coil of silky rope.

"Time to climb!" Max said.

"Just like gym class," Julie said.

Max and Neal leaped upward easily, tying the spider silk to rocks and ledges wherever they could.

"Last one up is a rotten bug egg!" Max squeaked, scurrying faster.

"Hey!" Neal complained, scrambling after him.

Keeah smiled, tightened her belt, grasped the rope, and pulled herself up. "Better hurry."

Without wasting a second more, Eric and Julie began their climb.

Strong winds battered them as they climbed higher and higher. They reached

one ledge after another without stopping. There wasn't time.

Soon they lost sight of the beach below.

"Careful," Julie said, joining Neal, Max, and Keeah on a narrow ledge. "Remember what the flies said. The groggles are up here. That means the Ninns are close by. They're not exactly going to welcome us."

"We're heading into danger," Keeah added.

Eric's heart raced. He stopped to catch his breath. "Why are the tiny creatures friendly and the big, powerful ones mean? Answer me that."

Neal, clinging to the ledge above, turned. "Size has *nothing* to do with power," he said.

Keeah smiled. "Let me guess, the flies told you that?"

"Nope. I made it up myself," said Neal

with a chuckle. "It must be the bug in me talking."

Kaww! Kaww!

Sudden cries echoed down the mountain.

"Groggles!" Keeah shouted. "Take cover!"

Everyone huddled under the ledge.

Everyone except Eric. He tried to pull himself up to where the others were. "Wait for me!"

But the groggles wouldn't wait. With a loud flapping noise, two of the big flying lizards swooped out of the sky, spotted Eric, and dived right for him.

"Go away, you ugly creeps!" Julie shouted. They all started pelting the groggles with rocks.

Kaww! Kaww!

One groggle shrieked, then pulled away.

But the second circled around for Eric again.

"Leave me alone!" Eric yelled, flailing his arms.

"More rocks!" Max cried, tossing handfuls of stones at the beast.

But the groggle kept dodging them.

Its sharp claws dug and scratched at one end of the ledge Eric was clinging to.

The rocks began to break away, tumbling down the mountain to the trees below.

"Oh, man!" Eric groaned. "Get me out of here!" He glanced to his left. The ledge narrowed to nothing only a few feet from him. On his right, the groggle was ripping the mountain away in huge clawfuls.

There was nowhere for him to go.

His friends kept throwing rocks at the beast.

"Hold on, Eric!" Neal shouted to him.

But Eric couldn't hold on.

There was nothing to hold onto.

Kaww! Kaww! The groggle lunged again.

The ledge crumbled away.

Eric grasped wildly at the air.

He fell.

Seven

The Glove of Power

"Nooooo!" Eric screamed.

The earth seemed to swoop up at him as he plummeted toward the jungle. In seconds he would crash into the treetops.

Suddenly something hard and bony wrapped around him. It tightened on his waist. It was a groggle's thick claw grasping him tight.

"Let me go!" Eric cried as the lizard

lifted him high into the air. "Well . . . I mean, don't actually let me go, but —"

Kaww! Kaww! the huge beast shrieked.

"— let me go!"

The groggle flapped quickly past Eric's friends. They yelled something out to him, but he couldn't hear what it was.

"Probably good-bye!" Eric groaned, twisting in the groggle's grip.

The beast soared up the mountain, then slowed and hovered over a broad, flat ridge.

Looking down, Eric could see a large mound of sticks and other junk in the middle of the ridge. The pile had a dip in the center.

"A nest!" he whispered to himself. "Please don't eat me!"

Kaww! The groggle swooped over the nest. It loosened its claws and dropped Eric.

"Oomph!" he groaned when he hit bottom. The groggle circled once, then flew off.

"Probably going to tell his friends that lunch is ready. Yeah? Well, no way!"

Eric scrambled to his feet. The thick nest surrounded him like a huge bowl. The walls of it, he figured, were about ten feet high. He could get out fairly easily.

"And I sure can't stay here!"

Eric dug his right foot in and hoisted himself up with his tired arms.

The nest was made of tangled branches and vines. In with them Eric noticed strips of polished wood and red-and-yellow cloth.

He knew what they were.

The remains of Keeah's ship.

"Robbers!" he snarled. Then he noticed something else. Something shiny and black. He stopped climbing. He peered down.

"The armored glove . . ." he whispered. He leaned into the branches, untangled the glove, and dragged it out. Carefully, he turned it over.

The setting for the jewel was broken.

The Red Eye of Dawn was not there.

Crack!

Eric froze. Sounds were coming from outside the nest. He crept up the rest of the way and peered over the top.

He laughed. He waved.

"Eric!" Neal squeaked, scrambling over the top of the ledge. The others followed close behind. Eric jumped from the nest and ran to meet them.

"We're safe," Keeah said, "but not for long. The groggles made such an incredible fuss that now the Ninns are coming."

"Oh, man!" Eric said. "Can't we ever get a break?"

Clomp! Clomp! A pack of fat Ninn soldiers hustled around the other side of the broad ledge.

"Guess not!" Neal yelped. "Yikes!"

Max squeaked. "May I suggest we go the opposite way?"

"You get my vote!" said Julie.

The heavy red warriors wasted no time, either.

They quickly loaded their bows.

"Aim!" one of them shouted.

"Yikes again!" Neal squeaked. "Duck everyone!"

"Fire!" the Ninns yelled.

Thwang! Thwang! Flaming arrows whizzed by the kids. They skidded along the ground and crashed against the rocks. The Ninns growled and reloaded.

"Hey, Ninns, let me give you a hand!" Eric shouted. He threw the armored glove right into the center of the pack of Ninns.

The fat warriors paused to look at it.

"And we're out of here!" Julie yelled.

The kids dashed around the nest to the far side of the ledge. Max shot in front, scampering as quickly as his eight legs could carry him. Neal raced right behind him.

They circled around the side of the mountain.

"A cave!" Neal said. "I see a cave!"

"I saw it first!" Max chirped.

They all leaped through the mouth of the cave and ran inside. They dashed into the shadows and held their breath.

Max held up one of his legs. "Listen. The Ninns aren't following. We've lost them."

"I think there's a reason," Julie whispered.

Eric turned to look. "Oh, man!" he groaned. "Isn't there at least *one* place on this island that isn't dangerous?"

Coming out of the cave depths were several large fuzzy legs and long twitching feelers.

"Here we go again," Neal said with a sigh.

Sssss!

Eight

Cave of Bugs

Ssss! Ssss!

The kids huddled in the shadows as two large brown-shelled bugs clambered out from the back of the cave.

"Your family, Neal," Julie whispered.

The bugs hissed and groaned. Their feelers twitched in the air. Then the kids saw why.

In the thin light streaming from the cave's opening, they saw a giant pit.

A giant pit full of eggs.

Julie sighed. "Been there, done that."

Sssss! The bugs hissed again more loudly than before. Their tongues flicked at the eggs.

"Listen, people," Neal whispered. "The bugs don't see us yet. Maybe we should just fight the Ninns, one on one."

"Ten on one, you mean," Max chittered.

"Holy cow," said Eric. "There it is!"

He pointed to the pit full of round pink eggs. One egg was smaller than the rest.

It was shiny.

It glowed bright red.

And it was shooting off sparks.

"The Red Eye of Dawn!" Keeah whispered. "My gosh! We found it!"

The bugs circled the pit, hissing and flicking.

Julie bit her lip. "Can't they tell the

glowing red one with all the sparks is not an egg?"

"They're bugs," Neal snorted. "They aren't that smart. Believe me, I know."

The red jewel sparkled again.

"Now I'm sorry I threw the glove away," Eric said. "How are we even going to touch that thing? It'll burn us for sure."

Keeah shook her head slowly. "Maybe there's a way. Galen said it was Sparr's anger that makes the Eye dangerous."

Neal's three eyes stared at the Eye. "And that means . . . ?"

"I know," said Julie. "It's like, if *you're* angry, the *Eye* is angry."

Eric nodded. "And maybe if you're the opposite of angry, the Eye won't shoot those deadly red beams everywhere."

"What's the opposite of angry?" Neal asked. "Being happy? Like laughing and stuff?"

Sssss! The bugs hissed and flicked again.

"That's the problem," Keeah whispered. "I don't feel happy. I just feel scared."

Julie turned to Neal. "Do bugs get scared?"

"Don't look at me," he replied. "I've been blasted once already. Besides, you definitely do *not* want to smell fried insect."

"No, it's my job," said Keeah. "I'm a wizard, sort of, halfway, at least."

"But how will you get past *them*?" Max said, nodding toward the bugs.

Julie held up her finger. "Wait, I have a plan."

"What plan?" Eric asked.

"The one where Neal pretends to be their baby bug. You know, to distract them."

Neal backed up as far as he could. "I

don't think so! I may be a dumb insect, but I'm not *that* dumb!"

"But, Neal," whispered Julie, "they'll be so excited to see you, Keeah can grab the jewel. It'll be perfect."

"Perfectly nuts!" Neal grumbled. "They'll lick me with those creepy tongues! No way!"

"We need the Eye to help free Galen," Keeah said. "Only Galen can make you yourself again."

Neal was quiet. His feelers twitched and quivered. He cleared his throat with a tiny cough. "Myself again? Really?"

"Plus, it'll be funny," said Eric. "Keeah will laugh so we won't blow up."

Neal sighed. "I guess so. But next time, someone else can be the bug!"

He fluttered his feelers once, took a squeaky breath, then scuttled out of the shadows.

"Mama! Papa!" he cried. "I'm home!"

The big bugs swung around, opened their feelers wide, and lunged for Neal. *Yeeeee!*

Keeah laughed as she scurried to the eggs.

The bugs completely surrounded Neal, squealing with delight.

"Hurry!" Neal yelled. "They're licking!"

Keeah laughed harder. Her hands closed firmly around the glowing red jewel.

"She's got it!" Max chirped. "And it's not shooting red bolts!"

"Neal," Eric cried. "Get out of there!"

In a flash, the five friends dashed out of the cave. The bugs hissed and squealed, but the kids shot around the ledge and up the side of the mountain before they could catch up.

Higher and higher they went, until there wasn't any more mountain to climb.

They crawled over the last rise.

A sharp wind passed over them.

They found themselves standing under a dark, open sky.

They were on the edge of a white cliff overlooking the vast sea of Droon.

Galen was there, wrapped in chains.

A hundred Ninns were there, guarding him.

And Lord Sparr was there, too.

"Give me the jewel . . . or die!" he snarled.

"Uh . . . is there a third choice?" Neal asked.

At once — *whoom!* — a wall of raging flames shot up around the kids.

"Trapped again," said Eric.

Nine

At the White Cliff

The kids huddled together to avoid the flames.

"A prison of fire," Sparr said. "You may thank Witch Demither for the idea. Thoughtful, isn't she?"

"My happy mood is fading fast," Keeah whispered. The wall of fire edged closer.

"Let them go," Galen boomed, struggling against his chains.

"Give me the Eye and you may all go,"

Sparr told them. He snapped his fingers, and one large Ninn raised his heavy sword. "Your chains will be cut, Galen. You will be free."

Max's eight legs trembled. "D-d-don't trust him."

Eric looked up. The flames coiled high into the air. The strange, green-winged sea-flies were beginning to gather above them.

Eric felt something wasn't right.

What was it?

Sparr stared through the flames. "I created the Red Eye of Dawn centuries ago to do my will —"

"Your evil will!" Keeah said, trying to remain calm. "All you do is put curses on people. Like Demither. Like my mother!"

Eric kept staring at their prison of fire. Demither's fire. He recalled how she had said once that she was a friend to no one, not even to Sparr.

The flames slithered over one another. They gleamed red, then silver, then red again. The Ninns were afraid of the fire. They wouldn't come close.

But still, something was wrong.

Zzzz! The seaflies buzzed lower.

Then, in a flash, Eric knew what it was. The fire looked hot enough to burn them to a crisp. But no smoke was coming from the fire. And no heat. The flies would never buzz so close if there was heat. That was it! The fire wasn't real.

It only *looked* hot.

The fire was . . . something else.

In fact, it was *hundreds* of something elses!

Sparr circled the flames. Soon, he would guess. Demither had tricked him.

In an instant, Eric formed a plan. He tapped Neal with his foot and glanced up at the seaflies. Then he nodded at the Ninn with the sword. "Can your pals do some-thing?"

Neal smiled a big smile. He twitched his feelers. Slowly, the flies lifted and buzzed over to the Ninn.

"Give me the Eye!" Sparr demanded.

"Get ready to move," Eric whispered. He stepped to the wall of fire.

"Eric, what are you doing?" Julie said.

"Just follow me." He held out his hand.

"Master Eric, no!" cried Max.

"Now!" Eric shouted.

Neal twitched, and the flies surrounded the fat Ninn. "Ugh!" the guard growled, swatting the flies. His heavy sword dropped to the ground.

At the same instant, Eric leaped through the fire. He was ready to scream, but he didn't have to. The instant he stuck his hand in, the flames ran over his fingers. The fire was icy cold!

"Silfs! I knew it!" he cried. The strange creatures spilled in a shower to the ground.

"Demither has betrayed me!" Sparr cried.

Eric and Julie dashed over and grabbed the Ninn's sword. Together they swung hard.

Chung! Galen's heavy chains fell away.

"Now you will pay!" Sparr shouted.

"No, Sparr," Keeah cried. "You will pay for the curses you have put on people!"

Ka-whoom! Bright beams shot wildly from Keeah's hand.

A terrible bolt blasted the ground near the Ninns, sending them rushing in every direction.

Another exploded near Neal.

"Oww!" he cried, as he leaped for cover.

"Keeah!" Galen shouted. "You cannot

control the Eye. Your anger will destroy you!"

"Throw it away!" Max yelled.

Keeah hurled the burning stone at the sea.

"IT IS MINE!" Sparr cried. He sucked in his breath and seemed to grow to twice his size. His eyes flashed, and his fins turned black with rage. He grasped his magic staff.

Ka-bam! Bolts of fire leaped from the staff. They shot across the air to the Eye. And the jewel stopped its fall to the sea. Slowly, it moved back toward Sparr.

"You see? The Red Eye of Dawn knows its master!" he howled. "Come to me, my jewel!"

Laughing, he reached for the sparking jewel.

Suddenly — *KA-WHOOOM!*

The peaceful sea exploded, and a giant serpent rose from the waves.

"Witch Demither!" Eric said.

The serpent reared her head and opened her jaws. "I am Demither, queen of oceans!"

And with a single lunge of her scaly arm, the witch closed her claws over the Red Eye of Dawn.

"No!" Sparr cried out. "Black was the day you were born, Witch Demither! I will find you!"

The serpent reared once more, then plunged into the water below, sending up a wave that crashed against the cliff like an exploding bomb.

"Awesome!" Julie gasped, staring at the water.

The sorcerer leaped upon a groggle and soared over the white cliff. "Ninns, follow me!"

Then, turning to Eric and his friends, Sparr cried, "Weak humans! You will end your days on this island! Crumble, earth! Fall to the sea!"

And the ground began to quake.

Ten

A Ship Reborn

Kaww! Kaww! The entire army of Ninns streaked across the sky after Lord Sparr.

The whole island rumbled and shook. Giant cracks split the rocks along the cliff.

"Let's get out of here!" Neal yelled, stumbling across the ground to his friends.

Eric gasped when he saw his friend. "Hey, Neal, you're back!"

"What's wrong with my back?" Neal said.

"It's normal!" Julie said. "You're Neal again! Not a bug! The Eye must have blasted you back to your regular you!"

"I always did like me!" Neal said. "Let's go!"

Rrrrr! The ground rumbled again and again.

"This way!" Galen urged. "The island is crumbling into the sea! Swiftly now!"

The six friends ran as quickly as they could down the white cliffs. They pounded through the tangled jungle. Rocks slid and crashed all around them. Trees fell in their path.

Finally, they reached the shore.

Krrrk! The giant white cliff above them began to split.

"We need a ship!" Keeah said.

Galen frowned. "We need something to

start us off. Something to build a ship with."

Eric's eyes went wide. "I know!" He ran across the beach. There, hidden in the rocks, were the wooden planks and torn sail from the old ship.

"Can we use these?" he asked breathlessly.

"Yes!" said Keeah.

Quickly, they assembled as much of the old ship as they could find. Together Galen and Keeah spoke fantastic words over them.

Suddenly, magically, the broken planks became hundreds of planks. Torn bits of sail furled upward into red-and-yellow squares of cloth.

The *Jaffa Wind*, more beautiful than ever, rose up before them.

"Hurry aboard," Max pleaded.

The moment they piled on, the giant

sails filled with wind, and the ship began to slide over the water.

KRRRK! A large crack tore open the cliff face, sending huge rocks tumbling to the sea below.

"Just in time!" Eric said.

The beach and the jungle were swept away by the crashing waves.

A moment later, the towering mountain itself fell into the sea. The mysterious island vanished.

As if it had never existed.

The ship sped magically over the waves.

Leaning against the side, Eric let out a long breath. "Sparr lost today," he said.

Keeah smiled. "Yes. For now, he doesn't have the Red Eye of Dawn. Now my father and I can search for my mother."

"What will Sparr do next?" Neal asked.

Galen glanced across the water. "Demither is heading north," he said, "to the coast of Mintar where she became what she became. Sparr will follow her there. But that is a story for another day. Look . . ."

The sun peered through the dark clouds and shone over the sea. It was a new day.

"And look at that," Neal said. "A city!"

They all ran to the upper deck. Rising in the distance were the silvery towers of an enormous city. Sunlight glimmered on the harbor and on the many colorful boats sailing into it.

"Jaffa City," Keeah exclaimed. "The capital of Droon. Home."

"We're home, too," Julie said. "There are the stairs." She pointed off the left side of the ship. The magic stairs were hovering over the calm waves.

A few minutes later, Neal, Julie, and Eric stepped from the ship onto the bottom stair.

"I have no words to thank you," Keeah said, "except to say — come back soon!"

"Droon needs such good friends as you," Galen said with a smile.

Eric smiled, too. "As long as the magic keeps working, we'll keep coming."

Julie hugged Keeah. "You can count on it."

"Farewell, Master Neal," said Max. "It was fun not being the smallest one, for a change."

Neal put his fingers to his forehead and wiggled twice. "That means — see you soon!"

The three children waved and raced up the stairs to the basement above them. They turned to look one last time at Keeah's ship as it sped over the sparkling sea to Jaffa City.

Then Eric flicked on the light.

Whoosh! The stairs vanished below them, and the gray cement floor appeared in its place.

"That was so strange," Eric said.

"The weirdest ever," Neal agreed.

They entered the basement.

Julie sighed. "But, somehow, I can't wait until we go again."

"Me, either," said Eric. "I wonder where we'll be next time. Jaffa City? The coast of Mintar?"

Neal made a face. "As long as they don't have bugs! Anyway, as Galen said, that's a story for another day. Look."

The soccer ball was lying on the workbench.

It was a normal ball once again.

Light flashed in through the basement windows. But it wasn't lightning. It was the sun.

"The storm's over," Eric said. Then he turned to his friends. "Anybody hungry?"

Neal grinned and twitched his fingers. "That means — you better believe it!"

Then they all ran up to the kitchen for lunch.

City
in the
Clouds

by Tony Abbott
Illustrated by Tim Jessell

To Debbie O'Hara
with love

One

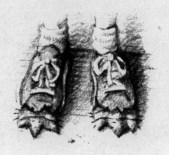

A Spell Returns

School was over for the day.

Eric Hinkle and his two best friends, Neal and Julie, climbed onto the bus home.

"It's been two whole weeks since we've been to you-know-where," Julie whispered as they squeezed into a seat together.

Eric smiled. Of course he knew where.

Droon, the totally secret and magical world of adventure that they had found under his basement.

"It's so strange," Eric said when the bus started up. "We have all these amazing new friends and we can't even talk about them."

"Enemies, too, don't forget," Neal added.

That was true. Since their first adventure in Droon, they had met Galen Longbeard, an old and powerful wizard, and his spidery helper, Max. Khan, king of the pillow-shaped purple Lumpies, had helped them, too.

But their special friend was Princess Keeah, a junior wizard who was trying to keep the wicked Lord Sparr and his red-faced Ninns from taking over her world.

"I wonder what Keeah is up to," Eric said. "I'm itching to go back."

"And I'm just itching!" Neal groaned, bending over suddenly to scratch his legs.

"In fact, I've been doing weird stuff all day. Not to mention the tiny little voices I keep hearing . . ."

That's when it happened.

Pop!

"Whoa!" Eric gasped, looking under the seat. "Look at that!" He pointed at Neal's sneaker.

Neal bent down. His shoelaces stretched and broke, one after another. The toe burst open and something brown and shiny popped out.

"Neal," said Julie, "what's with your sneaker? Is that the stuffing coming out?"

Eric gasped. "No, that's his foot coming out!"

"That's not my foot," said Neal. "It looks like a bug . . . a bug. . . . Wait. That *is* my foot! I've got a bug foot! Oh, no! I'm a bug again!"

The other kids on the bus turned and laughed.

Julie dropped her backpack over Neal's shoe before anyone saw it.

"Holy cow!" Eric whispered. "I know what's going on! Neal, brace yourself. It's back."

Neal frowned. "What's back?"

"The bug spell," he said.

"What?" Neal moaned. "I thought that spell was over!"

"It looks like it just came back," said Julie.

On their last adventure in Droon, a magic spell had gone wrong and accidently Neal had been turned into a bug.

A baby bug, with a hard brown shell, six legs, and feelers on his head that curled and twitched.

And now it was happening again.

Errr! The bus stopped, and the doors swung open.

"There's only one place to go," Eric said, grabbing Neal and pulling him off the bus. "To my basement. Hurry. We need to go back to Droon."

Together, they ran across the yard to Eric's house.

"The spell's not finished somehow," Julie said, frowning. "But don't worry, Neal. Droon is the most magical place ever. We'll find the cure."

"This is *not* going to last forever," Eric added.

"Forever?" Neal squealed. "Yikes!"

They hurried to the side door and opened it. Eric put his finger to his lips. "Nobody can see you like this, Neal." He paused to listen.

Julie nodded. "Let's be as quiet as —"

"A bug?" Neal said. "I can do that."

Eric listened to the clacking of a computer keyboard. "My mom's working." Then he called out. "Mom, I'm home. Neal and Julie are with me. We're going downstairs! Bye!"

They rushed through the kitchen.

On the way, Neal wiped some crumbs off the table, then licked his palm. "Sorry," he said. "Crumbs suddenly seem tasty to me."

Eric was worried. "I don't like this," he said. "Nothing magical has ever happened outside my basement . . . until now."

"Let's think about that *after* Neal's cured," said Julie. She shut the door behind them. They hustled downstairs.

"Now," she said, "did anybody dream of Droon?"

Eric shook his head.

Usually, a dream would call the kids to Droon.

Or the soccer ball in Eric's basement would turn into a globe of Droon. Princess Keeah had put a charm on it.

But the magic soccer ball was lying as usual on the workbench. It was just a ball.

"No dreams," Neal said. "Unless you count the one where I thought a lizard would eat me."

Julie shot Eric a worried look. "That's good enough. Come on."

They went to a door under the basement stairs.

Eric quickly opened the door and turned on the light. Everyone piled into a small room. He closed the door behind them.

"Ready?" he asked.

Neal held up his right hand. His fingers had started to form a claw. "I don't know about you, but I am!"

Julie flicked off the light.

Whoosh! The floor vanished instantly and the magic stairs appeared. Without wasting another moment, Eric darted down the steps.

Each time he and his friends had gone to Droon, the stairs had taken them somewhere different. He wondered where the stairs would lead this time.

"I see clouds!" Julie said. "We're in the air!"

Rrrr. A rumbling sound came from the clouds.

"Sounds like something is coming," Neal said.

Suddenly, the clouds parted. A round silver shape passed slowly under the bottom step.

"Whoa! It's some kind of huge flying thing," Julie said. The rainbow-colored stairs began to ripple under them.

"As usual, the stairway is fading too soon," Eric said. "We'd better jump." Then he gripped his friends' hands firmly.

Together, they jumped.

Plink! Plonk! Plunk! They landed on the ship.

"There's a hatch over there!" Julie shouted.

Freezing wind blew over them as they crawled across the silver surface to a small door.

Eric tried to open the hatch. "It's locked!"

Neal leaned over. He gripped a corner of the hatch with his clawed hand and twisted.

Krrnch! The little door sprang open to reveal a metal ladder running down inside the ship.

"At least being a bug makes me strong!" Neal said. "Let's go!"

One by one, the three friends went down into the strange flying ship.

Two

The Silver Ship

Eric reached up, grabbed the twisted hatch, and pulled it down over them. "Okay, we're on a flying ship. But whose flying ship? And where is it going?"

They looked around. They were in a narrow corridor. The walls were made of the same shiny metal as the outside of the ship.

"My bug senses are returning," said Neal. Then he pointed ahead of them.

"I hear voices this way. But I can't tell who."

"Let's find out," said Julie.

Carefully, they crept along the corridor. Neal's bug foot clomped on the floor. Eric followed behind.

They rounded a corner in the narrow hall.

Julie stopped. "Uh-oh . . ."

Hanging on the wall ahead of them was a row of shiny black armor, glinting in the light.

"That's Ninn armor!" Eric said. "There are Ninns on board! Maybe even Lord Sparr!"

"We're in enemy territory, folks," Neal added.

The ship rumbled noisily around them. It seemed to be changing direction.

The three friends quietly inched their

way to a large metal door with a wheel on it.

"A Ninn-sized hatch," Eric whispered. "Here goes nothing." He turned the wheel and opened the hatch slightly.

They peered into a large circular cabin filled with Ninn warriors. The Ninns were working the giant ship's controls.

Eric shivered. His friends huddled closer.

One Ninn stepped over to a red chair. The kids couldn't see who was in the chair.

"King Zello and his daughter are heading for the city of Ro, my lord," the Ninn grunted. "What shall we do?"

"Set course for the valley!" snarled a familiar voice.

"It's Lord Sparr!" Eric whispered.

"Soon we shall have the magic diamonds — millions of them," the Ninn grunted happily.

"The diamonds will be useful," Sparr said. "But what I really seek in the city of Ro is a single word. . . ."

Eric frowned. *A word? What word?*

The pink clouds thinned as the giant ship began to slip down through them. The cabin windshield showed a world of white mountains. Here and there were slithering silver rivers. A broad, flat valley directly ahead was circled by forests of violet and blue trees.

The world of Droon.

Pop! Neal's other sneaker began to split.

"Oh, man!" Neal moaned loudly. Too loudly.

Sparr bolted up from his throne and turned around. His dark eyes flashed when he saw the children. "Spies! Seize them!"

Instantly, three large Ninns rushed over and grabbed the children.

The red guards' grips were like steel.

"Let us go, Sparr!" Julie exclaimed.

Sparr laughed. "That's exactly what I intend to do! Ninns, take them to the platform!"

The sorcerer's bald head gleamed as if it had been polished. And small dark fins grew behind each ear.

"Do you expect us to talk?" Eric asked.

"No, I expect you to . . . fly!" Sparr replied.

Without another word, the big red warriors hustled them roughly into the corridor.

"Where are you taking us?" Neal asked.

"You'll find out!" one Ninn laughed. He pressed a button on the corridor wall and — *whoosh!* — a door in the side of the ship opened.

The children found themselves on a small metal plank jutting out from the ship.

The wind howled around them.

"Okay," said Eric, "I'm guessing that this platform is not a good thing."

"We call it the tossing platform!" one of the guards said with a grunting sort of laugh. His black eyes seemed like tiny marbles in his puffy red face.

"We toss, you fly!" another Ninn said.

"And what if we can't fly?" Julie asked.

"Splat!" The third Ninn laughed.

The kids all looked at one another.

"Okay, now I'm worried," Neal said.

"And you weren't up till now?" Julie cried.

Suddenly — *zzzzzz-blam!* — the ship rocked.

Ka-blam! Boom! The sky lit up with sparkling blue beams. Dozens of plump purple ships swooped out of the clouds.

The ships were small and round and very fast. Two wings stuck out on each side of a clear bubble.

"The Lumpies!" Julie shouted.

The Ninns grunted and ran inside. The iron door closed behind them. The kids were trapped outside the ship.

"Now I'm really worried!" Neal said. "We really *are* going to go splat!"

Suddenly, one of the purple planes swept underneath the platform. It pulled up sharply. Its cockpit bubble opened. There were two figures inside. "Jump! Quickly!" yelled the pilot.

They did. "Oomph! — whoa! — yeow!"

The ship circled up and away into the pink clouds as the kids tumbled onto soft purple pillows. They landed right next to a small purple creature who looked like a chubby pillow himself.

The creature's cheeks bulged like bubblegum bubbles.

"Khan!" Eric cried.

"King of the Lumpies, at your service!"

Khan said, his short arms flying over the controls.

Zzzz — blam! The back end of the little ship roared with the sound of blasting. A helmeted creature behind them leaned over a strange gun.

Sparkling blue beams of light burst on the giant silver ship below. Sparr's airship changed direction and veered away.

"Lumpies one, Sparr zero!" Khan cheered.

"Nice blasting from your helper back there," Julie said to Khan. "Amazing, whoever that is!"

"She ought to be," Khan said with a twinkle in his eye. "That's Princess Keeah!"

Three

The Flying City of Ro

Princess Keeah tore off her helmet. Her long blond hair tumbled to her shoulders. "I'm so glad to see you!" she said. "We were on our way to meet my father when Sparr attacked us. But why are you here?"

Neal held up his claw. "The spell from last time sort of . . . came back."

"Oh, my!" the princess gasped.

"Plus," Eric added, "then we heard that

Sparr plans to steal diamonds from a place called Ro!"

Keeah glanced at the Lumpy leader.

"We have no time to waste," Khan muttered. He pulled on the lever and they soared up into the pink clouds.

"What's going on?" Julie asked.

Keeah turned to her friends. "My father and I were supposed to meet Galen and Max at the city of Ro to find out where my mother is."

Eric nodded. On one of their previous journeys, they had learned that Keeah's mother, Queen Relna, was not dead as everyone had thought. A witch had told them she was alive.

"Where is this city of Ro?" Julie asked.

"Everywhere!" Keeah answered. "Ro is a flying city. It flies constantly over all of Droon."

"Cool!" Neal said, scratching his neck.

"Very cool, as you say," Khan said. "And on any other day Sparr would not be able to attack it."

"Why is today so important?" Eric asked.

Khan pulled the purple ship higher. "Ro hides itself under a spell of invisibility."

"Except," said Keeah, "that one day each year Ro becomes visible. It lands in the Kalahar Valley to collect diamonds. The magic jewels hold the power of invisibility."

"Those are the diamonds Sparr is after," Julie said.

Eric was drawn to the small ship's front windscreen, where a large white bird soared along with the purple ship.

"The white falcon!" he said. He remembered all the times he'd seen it before in Droon.

Keeah smiled. "The falcon is always nearby, watching over what we do." Then she turned.

"Neal, I'm sorry the spell came back," she said. "But you're in luck. The Guardians live in Ro. They are very old and very wise. They know more than anyone about, well, anything! They can help you."

Khan sniffed. "But we must hurry. At midnight, Ro vanishes again. Once it does, it will be impossible to leave for a whole year!"

The small winged craft shot over a range of snowy mountains and dipped to a desert plain.

A few moments later, Khan landed on the outside of a ring of tall hills.

"The Kalahar Valley is beyond these hills," Keeah said, stepping from the ship. "Come."

As the sun lowered into afternoon, the

small band crept through a narrow pass in the hills.

"Oh, my gosh!" Julie exclaimed as they tramped out to a ledge on the other side.

The valley below teemed with hundreds of Ninn warriors. They were armed with bows and arrows and swords. With them were dozens of winged lizards called groggles.

Suddenly, a great cry rose up from the red warriors. They looked skyward to see Sparr's silver airship circling the valley.

But that was nothing compared to what happened next.

On the far side of the valley, the drifting pink clouds slowly parted.

Over the hills came a giant city. It looked as if it had been uprooted from the earth. Slowly, it floated downward into the center of the valley.

"Ro!" Keeah whispered excitedly. "I hope my father made it there safely. And Galen and Max, too."

"It's awesome," Eric exclaimed, looking up.

The city was built on an enormous floating disk that seemed to stretch for miles across.

Strangely shaped towers spiraled to the sky. Bridges soared from one side of the city to the other. Domes of green, pink, and blue topped buildings of every shape and size.

And the lights! The whole city gleamed and sparkled as if every inch of it were lit!

"Ro is a city of peace, ruled over by the wisest of people, the Guardians," Khan said.

"But now Sparr is waiting for it," Keeah said with a shiver.

The city finally rumbled to the ground, nestling into the valley as if it had always been there.

As soon as it landed, a white ray of light shot from the city to the valley floor.

"They are drilling for the diamonds," Khan whispered.

A moment later, millions of tiny glittering rocks flowed back through the light to the city.

"They're drilling with light," said Neal.

"How can we get in?" Eric asked. "There's an army of Ninns between us and the city."

The Lumpy king sniffed suddenly. The kids remembered that Lumpies were expert sniffers.

"We're in luck," the purple king said. "I smell a flock of wild groggles roosting nearby. And the Ninns don't know about them."

"Groggles?" Neal muttered. "Those flying lizards *eat* bugs like me. Anyone have a Plan B?"

"But Khan's a groggle whisperer!" Keeah said.

"A what?" asked Eric.

"I talk softly to them," Khan said with a chuckle. "And the groggles listen. The wild ones who live in the mountains are actually quite nice."

The five friends crept slowly up to a flock of groggles nesting on the edge of the valley.

In the sky above, Sparr's silver airship circled the giant city and swooped down into it. As if this were a signal, the Ninns jumped onto their own groggles. A moment later, Sparr's flying army swarmed up from the valley floor.

"Quickly now!" Keeah cried. "Ro will soon take flight."

"Psss!" Khan whispered soft words into one lizard's ear. It grunted, dipped for everyone to climb on its back, then lifted from the ground with a great flapping of wings.

With the kids clutching the groggle tightly, it soared up to join the others.

Four

Into the Palace

"Psss-psss-psss!" Khan whispered. The groggle obeyed, circling high over the city.

"There it is!" Keeah exclaimed. "The Guardians' palace has the tallest tower."

Below them stood a palace of shiny gray stone. From its top a tower coiled up to the sky. It was the tallest and strangest of all the buildings in the city.

The groggle landed clumsily on a small

street near the palace and the kids piled off. The streets were deserted.

"The people of Ro are peaceful," Khan said. "They will likely be hiding."

"First things first," said Eric. "We need to find a cure for Neal."

"No," said Neal. "First we stop Sparr."

"Finding the Guardians will help us do both," said Keeah.

Julie pointed into the air. "We'd better find them soon. Here comes Sparr's silver ship."

They watched from the corner as Lord Sparr's airship landed in a large square in front of the palace. Almost immediately, a hatch opened and Lord Sparr himself appeared.

"Princess Keeah," Khan whispered, "I will try to find your father and tell him where we are. With my nose, I should be able to sniff myself past Sparr and his chubby guards."

The kids wished the Lumpy king good luck.

Suddenly, the street beneath them rumbled. The stones vibrated under their feet.

"We're flying!" Neal said. "Ro is going up!"

They peered between the buildings to see the foothills slip away below them. The air grew colder. Clouds drifted over the rooftops. Ro was in the air once again.

"Let's roll!" Julie cried. "Before it's too late!"

The band of friends crept into the first hallway they could find. It was dark and cool.

"Okay," said Eric. "Where should we go?"

Keeah pointed into the darkness. "My

father says, when in doubt, head for the center."

"Looks kind of spooky in there," Julie said.

"I like the dark," said Neal. "I can actually see better. I hear voices, too. Not Ninns, though. I think this is the way."

They followed Neal deeper into the palace.

Julie turned to Keeah. "Why does Ro become invisible?"

"To protect the Tower of Memory," the princess answered. "Everything that happens in Droon is written in the Tower. The Guardians are keepers of the Tower and of the whole history of our world. My father and I hoped they might tell us what happened to my mother."

"Do you think they can help debug me?" Neal asked.

Keeah nodded. "That's my plan."

"Cool," said Neal. "Then that's my plan, too!"

Together, the four friends scurried up a set of steps to another level. They could still feel the city rising higher and higher into the air.

Strange noises echoed behind them.

Eric wondered if the Ninns were on their trail. Did Sparr already know they were there? And if he found them, what would he do? *Splat?*

"The Guardians rule over the people of Ro," Keeah added. "They're the last of a band of knights who have lived since the earliest days of Droon."

Suddenly, Neal stopped short and everyone bunched up behind him.

"What's the matter?" Eric asked.

"The hall ends here," his friend said.

"Well, that's dumb," said Julie. "Why would they have a hall that leads nowhere?"

Keeah chuckled. "The hall may end, but the way continues." In the dim light, she pointed to a strange mark on the wall above them.

"What is it?" Julie asked.

"It's an ancient language," Keeah said, peering close. "I don't know all the words, but I know this one. It means . . . the Guardians!"

Keeah pushed at the wall.

Vrrrt! It slid aside easily.

The children slipped through the opening.

They found themselves in a tall room with a curved ceiling.

"I should tell you one more thing about the Guardians," Keeah said. "They are —"

"Oh, my gosh!" Julie gasped.

"Whoa!" Eric grunted.

"I think we found where they keep the dinosaurs!" Neal whispered.

Five

The Guardians of Droon

In the center of the room were two seven-foot-tall lizards with large heads. They stood upright, swishing their heavy tails across the tiled floor.

Their short upper arms ended in six-inch-long clawed fingers. Their teeth were even longer.

But the strangest part was that they were dressed in shiny green robes.

"Let's . . . um . . . sneak back out," Eric said.

"Before they see us . . ." Julie added.

But Keeah walked slowly up to the creatures.

"Ah!" said one of the dinosaurs. "Princess Keeah and her friends from the Upper World!"

"Welcome to the city of Ro," the other said.

Eric blinked. "Are you . . . dinosaurs?"

"Theropods, actually," one said. "I'm Bodo."

"And I'm Vasa," said the other. "We're the Guardians!"

Bodo pulled a pair of spectacles from his robe and slipped them on. He stepped over to Neal. "You must be Neal, the boy with the problem."

Neal blinked. "How did you know my name?"

The creature smiled. "I was reading in the Tower this morning. I knew you were coming."

"Then you know that Sparr is here, too?" Keeah said. "And his Ninns are everywhere."

Vasa hissed between his teeth. "Sparr has come for the diamonds. He wants to harness their power for his own evil ends."

"Then we must hurry," Bodo said.

Vasa put a claw to his chin and walked around Neal. "Hmm. Yes, I see. We must find out exactly what happened the instant you became a bug. You must read what Quill has written about it in the Tower of Memory."

"Who is Quill?" Eric asked.

"Our magic feather," Vasa said. "All of Droon's history — all that has ever happened — Quill writes in the ancient language. He writes everything on the stones of the Tower."

"And sometimes," Bodo said with a chuckle, "Quill writes so fast, he gets ahead of himself."

Keeah frowned. "What do you mean?"

It was Vasa's turn to laugh. "He means that Quill writes what hasn't happened yet!"

"You mean . . . the future?" Eric asked.

"Oh, yes," Bodo replied. "But what we need now is from the past." He scribbled on a small square of paper and handed it to Neal.

On the paper was a strange drawing.

"What's this?" Neal asked.

"Your name, in the ancient language," Bodo replied. "And here are the rest of your names."

Eric   *Julie*   *Keeah*

The children took the papers from Bodo. He also gave them small writing tools that looked like pencils.

Vasa stepped over to Keeah. "But you, Princess, you are here for something else?"

She nodded. "My father and I were coming to see what you could tell us about where my mother is. We know she is alive . . . somewhere."

Vasa nodded slowly. "Queen Relna was — is — a great ruler, as is your father, King Zello."

Keeah breathed deeply and continued. "She fought Lord Sparr at the forbidden city of Plud. She was never seen again."

"Princess, you must look for this symbol."

"Your mother's name. Relna. Also this one."

"Who is that?" Julie asked.

"Lord Sparr," Eric said, though he wasn't sure why. "Am I right?"

Bodo and Vasa shared a look at each other, then nodded. "Indeed, you are correct, Eric."

Clang! Boom! Blam!

Bodo raised his claw. "Sparr has entered the palace! Go to the Tower quickly. Take these symbols. Read the characters next to them and bring back what you have found out. All your questions will be answered."

"But what about you?" Keeah asked.

"Sparr will not harm us today," Vasa said.

Clomp! Clomp!

"Ninns!" Neal hissed. "We're too late!"

"A simple spell will help you escape capture," Vasa said. He took a book from a nearby shelf and held it open. "Keeah, say these words."

Bodo nodded to Keeah. "Only a true wizard, even a young one, can perform spells. Hurry!"

Keeah began to read. "Bello . . . gum . . ."

Clomp! Ninn footsteps echoed just outside.

"Pello . . . mum . . ."

"What's going to happen?" Julie asked.

"Rello . . . hum!"

Fwoot — boomf — pahhh! The room filled with thick blue smoke just as the doors blasted open.

Light from a dozen blazing torches filled the small room. Ninn warriors entered and grabbed Bodo and Vasa roughly.

Then the doorway filled with a dark shape. Lord Sparr entered.

Eric expected the sorcerer to start screaming.

He'd toss the kids off the flying city. *Splat!*

Sparr strode over to Eric and his friends.

"My noble warriors," Sparr boomed. "How does the battle go?"

Eric blinked. He gasped. Then he looked over at Neal and Julie. He nearly choked when he saw their faces. They were thick and red. Their cheeks were all puffy. They growled with angry looks. Then he looked down at himself.

"Ungh!" he grunted.

Eric and his friends were . . . Ninns!

Six

Working for Lord Sparr

Eric tugged at the skin on his arm. It was rough and thick and oily. "Yuck," he muttered.

Neal, Julie, and Keeah pinched their skin, too.

"I'd rather be a bug!" Neal whispered.

"King Zello and the Lumpies have landed," Sparr said. "How is our attack going?"

"Um . . . really good," Neal said with a grunt.

"Good?" Sparr repeated.

"Lots of Lumpies ran away."

"And . . ." Sparr said.

"King Zello has fallen back," Keeah said, groaning in a deep voice as a Ninn might do.

"And the wizard, what's his name?" Julie boomed.

"Galen," Sparr said with a snarl.

Eric snorted. "Don't expect to see him for a while!"

Sparr smiled evilly. "You have done well. Go gather diamonds with the others." Then he turned to Bodo and Vasa.

Vasa hissed as Sparr approached. "You won't get away with this, Sparr . . ."

"Ah, yes, the Guardians," Sparr scoffed. "Last of the peace-loving knights of Droon's distant past. You are no threat to me, you . . . fossils!"

Bodo narrowed his lizardy eyes at the sorcerer. "Beneath the cloak of invisibility, Ro has prospered for centuries. Beneath the cloak of peace lies great power."

Lord Sparr's face went pale. "We shall see how powerful you are when I use your diamonds to create an invisible army!"

Then he snapped his fingers.

Another troop of Ninns wheeled in a long wooden cart brimming with the most dazzling white jewels Eric had ever seen.

Magic diamonds.

"Have you found them all?" Sparr growled.

The Ninn bowed his head. "Not all, my lord."

Eric looked at his own hands again. They were big and red and puffy, with six fingers. He started to feel sick. A wave of

dizziness came over him. He felt hot and cold at the same time.

His stomach rumbled.

Then he felt himself shrinking inside his Ninn armor. He was changing back!

He looked over at Julie, Neal, and Keeah. They, too, were beginning to change. In a moment, they wouldn't be Ninns anymore!

Eric grunted. Even his voice was changing.

Sparr flashed a look at him. "What is it?"

"We . . . um . . . better check on our groggles," he said, hoisting up his leather pants, which were beginning to slip down on him. "Gotta give them biscuits or they get mad."

Sparr squinted. "Biscuits?"

"Um, right!" Keeah blurted out, her

voice not so deep anymore. "Then we'll go find those pesky kids. And that princess. You know, the junior wizard. She's powerful, but we can take her."

Eric's eyes gaped. He nudged Neal. Neal's foot was turning back into a bug foot.

"If you find the children, throw them off the side!" Sparr boomed. "Go! We leave Ro soon!"

Neal grabbed Eric, Julie, and Keeah. They clomped out the door and ran until they were out of breath.

"Bodo and Vasa could have told us we were on a timer!" Eric exclaimed when they were far away from the Guardians' room.

Julie bit her lip. "We need to split up. You guys head to the Tower and find Neal's cure. I'll see if I can help Bodo and

Vasa. We'll meet at the front steps in an hour."

"Half an hour," Keeah said. "Ro will disappear very soon. Look."

They all looked out a window in the hall. Outside the palace, the sky was turning a deep blue. The moon shone through puffy white clouds.

"It's nearly midnight," Keeah said. "We haven't much time."

"I'll go with Julie," Neal said. "My bug sense may help us stay away from Ninns. Real Ninns."

"Neal, you'll be normal again soon," Eric said, patting his friend on the back. Then he stopped. Neal's back was as hard as a shell.

Eric swallowed hard.

Neal was getting worse. Much worse.

"Come on, Keeah," Eric said. "To the Tower!"

The gang split up. With Ninn footsteps echoing all around them, Eric and Keeah threaded their way toward the center of the palace.

To the giant Tower of Memory.

Seven

Written in Stone

The Tower of Memory was a huge spiral of stones coiling up from the ground.

Eric and Keeah entered a vast inner courtyard, looked up, and saw it.

"It's huge," Eric whispered.

Row upon row of rough gray blocks circled higher and higher into the starlit sky.

"Do you have the papers with our

name symbols?" Keeah said, spotting a narrow opening in the tower.

"Yes." Eric clutched Neal's square of paper, along with his own and Julie's. "Let's do it."

They slipped through the opening.

The inside of the tower was empty and very quiet. The only noise was a faint scratching sound from above.

Eric squinted up. There, on the very top row of stones, barely visible in the mist and moonlight, was the magic feather, Quill. It scratched word after word into the stones, writing quickly, then stopping, then writing faster than ever.

Whenever it filled one stone with the strange words and symbols, another stone mysteriously appeared next to it. Quill filled that one and went on to another. And another.

"This is so weird," Eric said softly. "The

Tower is building itself. It keeps getting taller."

"Quill writes what happens to everyone," Keeah said. "Everything that has ever happened in Droon is right here."

"And some things that haven't happened yet."

Eric turned a complete circle as he followed the rows of silvery gray stones, looking for the strange symbols the Guardians had given them.

Keeah breathed out suddenly.

"What?" Eric said, turning to her.

"My mother's symbol!" she said, running to the wall nearest her. "And Sparr's! I see them. That must be it! What happened to her at Plud!"

She began scratching down the strange words with the pencil Bodo had given her.

Then Eric saw his own name among the carvings. "Oh, wow!"

Next to it were Julie's and Neal's names. He scanned the lower rows to see if the names appeared before then. No, they didn't. But their names were written many times after that. He looked up as far as he could. Their names were still there, curving into the upper rows.

All the way into the future?

Would he and his friends do many things in Droon? Eric wished he could read the top row, to find out what the future might bring. He, too, started scribbling down the strange words for the Guardians to decipher.

Keeah uttered something softly. Eric turned to see her slip quietly out of the Tower.

He was about to call out to her, then

stopped. The hair on the back of his neck stiffened. He knew someone else was in the Tower with him.

Slowly, Eric turned his head. There, standing in the exact center of the room, was a tall, dark figure. A man.

Eric gasped to himself.

The man was Lord Sparr.

Sparr stood motionless, reading the walls of the Tower and mumbling the words to himself. As he did, tears welled in his eyes, glinting in the moonlight from the Tower's top opening.

One tear trickled down Sparr's cheek. He flicked it away instantly. The teardrop hit the stone floor, hissing on the cold stones. *Ssss!*

"Oh, whoa!" Eric breathed.

Suddenly Quill began scratching on the stones more speedily than before. Eric remembered what the Guardians had said.

Sometimes Quill writes so fast, he writes what hasn't happened yet.

Sparr raised his eyes toward a single spot on the upper walls.

As Eric watched, the sorcerer lifted off the ground and flew up to the top of the Tower.

Quill kept scratching faster and faster. He filled one stone after another.

Eric knew. Quill was writing the future.

An instant later, Sparr was back.

Eric could not move, could not breathe. It seemed like hours that Sparr just stood there.

Then, a strange sound came from the sorcerer. A sound like all his breath leaving him.

And out of that breath came a single word.

"Ice."

Sparr began to laugh softly.

Eric felt as if he would explode. He needed to sneeze. Then cough. He felt as if he couldn't hide a second longer. And yet he had to be quiet. Or Sparr would see him and hurt him. *Splat!*

Just then, a white shaft of moonlight suddenly fell into the Tower from the opening above. Eric pressed himself back against the stones, but the shaft of light moved across the floor to him.

Sparr turned instantly. His eyes flashed red.

He saw Eric. He stared right at him!

Clomp! Clomp! A troop of Ninns tramped into the tower. "It is time, Lord Sparr," one said.

The moonlight dimmed behind a cloud and Eric was in shadow once more.

Sparr nodded. "I have seen what I came here for."

Sparr was still staring at Eric. He could destroy Eric in a second!

Then why?

Why?

Why did Sparr simply wrap his long black cloak around him and walk out of the Tower?

Eight

Neal and Company

Clomp! Clomp! The Ninns tramped through the halls and out of the palace.

Sparr went with them.

"Eric!" Keeah ran back into the tower. "I was so scared when you didn't follow me."

Eric nodded slowly. "I couldn't move," he said. "Sparr saw me, but . . . he let me go."

Keeah's eyes widened. "Eric, we need

to get back to the Guardians. Ro will disappear soon, and we'll disappear with it."

They rushed back to the Guardians' room. The Ninns had gone. Vasa and Bodo were free.

"Neal and Julie have gone to see where Sparr is taking the diamonds," Vasa said quickly. "What did you find in the Tower?"

Trembling, Keeah handed her paper to them.

"Ah, the secrets of Droon's past," Bodo said.

Vasa peered over his shoulder and began to translate what Keeah had written. "At the city of Plud, Lord Sparr nearly killed Queen Relna."

"But, you see," Bodo went on, "the witch Demither put a curse on Relna. Instead of suffering death, the queen assumed an animal form."

Keeah gasped. "An animal? Is it . . ."

"Yes," Bodo said, squinting at the words. "A white bird. A falcon."

"I knew it!" Keeah cried, jumping for joy. "That's why the falcon is always there! It's my mother following me, watching over us!"

"But Demither told us the queen was in prison," Eric said.

"True," Vasa went on. "Such a curse is a kind of prison. But now the queen needs your help if she is ever to be human again. Hers is a dangerous journey, filled with many trials."

Keeah wiped away a tear. "I will help her."

"So will we," said Eric, smiling at the princess.

Vasa turned to Eric, "And what did you discover?"

Eric gulped as he handed the paper to Vasa. "Sparr saw me, but he just . . . walked away."

Bodo glanced at Vasa, then peered through his spectacles at Eric. "And you have a question."

Eric nodded. "Does what Quill writes *have* to happen? I mean, can the future be *changed*?"

"We won't know that until the future becomes the present," said Bodo.

Eric frowned. "But . . ."

Suddenly, Julie and Neal rushed into the chamber.

"The diamonds are being loaded into Sparr's airship!" Julie said breathlessly. "He looks like he's leaving the city."

"And look at me," Neal said. "I'm getting way worse!" He held up his hands. They were both claws now.

"Quickly, Neal, stand here," said Vasa,

holding Eric's writing up to the light. To-gether with Keeah, the Guardians began to mumble strange words. "Timbo . . . limbo . . . koo-kimbo!"

Poomff! A huge ball of smoke appeared in the chamber. A moment later, Neal walked out.

He looked normal. He held up two nor-mal hands. His sneakers were still ripped, but human toes were sticking out. He broke into a smile.

"Yes!" he cried. "I am back!"

"Me, too!" cried another voice.

Everyone turned to see a second Neal emerge from the smoke.

"Uh-oh," said Keeah.

Two Neals walked around the room.

Twins!

"Ah, yes," Vasa said. "This is a normal side effect of the spell. Only temporary. Don't worry."

The first Neal smiled. "I always thought two Neals were better than one!"

"Slap me five, brother!" said the second.

Rrrrr! The walls began to shake.

"Ro is turning invisible again," Bodo said. "Go. This way is quickest!" He pointed to a secret door in the chamber.

"It leads to the square outside," Vasa added. "Good luck to you all! May you find your mother, Princess. And farewell to you, Neal."

"Thanks!" said Neal.

"Same here!" said the other.

Eric, Keeah, Julie, and the two Neals rushed through the door and outside the palace.

Clomp! Clomp! The square was crawling with Ninns. They were loading the diamonds into the cargo area of Sparr's silver ship.

"We've got to get those back!" Keeah said.

"And I've got to find out why Sparr let me go," Eric whispered.

"Does anybody have a plan?" Julie asked.

"I've got a plan!" boomed a strange, loud voice from the shadows nearby. "How about we form a human wall and blast our way in!"

"Wh-wh-who is that?" Keeah whispered.

The shadows stirred and out stepped a large man with bright green armor. He had a helmet with horns on it. He carried two wooden clubs.

"Whoa!" one Neal mumbled.

"A Viking!" said the other.

"No, that's my daddy!" Keeah exclaimed, running to the man and giving him a hug. She twirled around. "Meet my father — King Zello!"

The king smiled a huge grin. "Khan found me. Galen and Max are here, too."

The old wizard stepped from the shadows. He was dressed in long blue robes. "I am pleased that you children are safe." He looked at the Neals. "All of you!"

Galen's spidery helper, Max, clambered along the wall to them. "The magic stairs have appeared in the Kalahar Valley. We must hurry."

Just then, the air around them became all wavy. The stones in the square seemed to wiggle and turn clear.

Max scrambled in a circle around the children. "It's happening!" he chittered nervously. "The flying city of Ro — is disappearing!"

King Zello hoisted his wooden clubs, one in each hand. "You kids get to the ship.

Galen and I will distract the Ninns. Yee-haw!"

The Ninns turned from the ship. They grunted. They charged across the square.

Eric looked at his friends. "Everyone to Sparr's ship! Now!"

The four friends ran for the cargo door. They leaped in.

Clang! The giant door on Sparr's airship slammed shut behind them.

Nine

Mountains of Diamonds!

They jumped to their feet and looked around.

"Holy cow!" Julie muttered.

All around them were piles, mounds, mountains of shimmering, glittering diamonds.

"With these Sparr could make his whole Ninn army invisible," Keeah said.

"He'd be unstoppable!" Neal exclaimed.

"That's why we have to stop him now," said Eric.

One Neal started shaking his head. "I don't like being locked in Sparr's personal ship. A few hours ago, we were trying to get out of here!"

"Yeah, shouldn't we try to keep the ship from flying away?" the other Neal asked.

Suddenly, the walls rumbled around them.

"We're taking off," Keeah said.

"I have an idea!" the first Neal said. He entered a corridor of the ship.

"Where are you going?" the second asked.

No answer.

"Man, he never listens!" Neal grumbled.

Then, just as in the Tower of Memory,

Eric sensed that they were not alone. He turned.

"Looking for me?" said a voice.

Lord Sparr stepped into the cargo bay.

Slowly, Eric made his way toward him. The fins behind Sparr's ears went from purple to black. His face was full of anger.

"Princess Keeah," he said. "Say good-bye to your beloved world. I have read the future. Droon shall soon be mine!" He raised his hand to her. Red light leaked from his fingertips.

Keeah tried to jump away, but she slipped on the floor. Without thinking, Eric leaped in front of her.

"Watch out!" Neal cried out, jumping in front of both of them.

At the same moment, the other Neal raced in. "What? Old fish fins hurting my friends? As if!"

And he jumped in front of the other Neal.

Sparr shot a blast at them all.

Zzzz! Poomf! The air went red.

Eric pushed Keeah out of the way at the same time as both Neals crashed into each other.

Sparr bolted away into the depths of the ship.

"I'll get you!" yelled Eric. In a flash, he was on his feet and down a corridor after the sorcerer. He chased Sparr into the main control cabin.

Eric screeched to a stop. Cold air was rushing into the cabin. Sparr stood near an open hatch.

"Stay where you are!" The sorcerer's eyes burned with rage. But he did not try to hurt Eric.

"You're keeping me alive, aren't you?" Eric said. "Why? For what? Tell me!"

Sparr grinned. "Because of what will happen. Because of how you will . . . help me!"

"What?" Eric cried. "I'll never help you!"

"Time . . . will tell!" the sorcerer said. Then he lifted his cloak behind him and leaped from the hatch.

Eric crawled to the opening in time to see Sparr spread his cloak and swoop to the ground.

"I'll never help you!" Eric yelled to the wind.

When he ran back to the cargo bay, everyone was shaking their heads.

"Oh, man!" Neal groaned. "This is the worst!"

"Neal?" Eric said. "Where's the other you?"

"When Sparr blasted us we came together," he said. "Poof! There's only me now. I'm normal."

Eric jumped up. "Yahoo! Just you? You're just you! This is terrific! Boy, are we happy!"

Neal frowned. "We would be except for . . ."

"Except for what?" Eric asked.

"Except for what he told me . . ."

"What who told you?"

"The other Neal. Right before *we* became *me*."

"What did he tell you?" Eric cried.

"That he did something to the ship —"

KA-BOOOOM! The walls shook with a tremendous blast, throwing the kids to the floor. Flames leaped up the outside of the ship. Smoke began to fill the cargo bay.

"That!" Neal yelled, grasping for something to hold onto. "The other Neal did *that*! So Sparr wouldn't get away."

"But his plan sort of backfired," Julie said.

The ship rocked again, then started to dip.

"Uh-oh," Eric said, "I think we're going down."

"We are definitely going down," said Keeah.

Neal frowned. "Splat, anyone?"

Ten

The Sorcerer's Power

The nose of Sparr's giant silver airship tipped forward sharply.

"We're going to crash!" cried Neal.

"We're not going to crash," said Eric. "Sparr could have hurt us but he didn't. He read the future in the Tower of Memory and he let us live. We'll get out of this somehow. I promise."

The ship dived even faster.

"Um . . . how?" Julie asked.

Vrrr! Vrrr! Outside the cargo bay windows a small purple wingship pulled up.

"Daddy and Khan and Max and Galen!" Keeah shouted. "They followed us!"

Eric grinned. "Told you we'd be okay."

Julie clambered over the mounds of diamonds and hit a button on the wall.

Whoosh! A door opened.

"The tossing platform!" she said.

They all climbed out. The Droon night was deep blue. Flames licked up the sides of the big ship as Khan pulled his small purple ship closer.

"It's now or never, folks!" Neal said.

Clutching one another's hands tightly, the four friends jumped from the flaming platform. They landed right in the cockpit of Khan's wingship.

"Now you are safe!" King Zello said, hugging his daughter tightly to him.

Vrrr! Khan roared up and away as the giant flaming hulk dived to the earth.

In the sky nearby, the last traces of Ro were fading. The tall, lizard-like people of the city were gathered in the square to wave at the purple ship.

"Good-bye, Guardians," Neal said. "Good-bye people of Ro. Thank you!"

Suddenly — *ka-whoom!* — Sparr's silver airship slammed into a snow-covered mountain. It exploded with a tremendous fiery blast. A cloud of black smoke rose from the wreckage.

At that instant, too, a white light shone down from the fading city. The light rippled once and diamonds — millions of diamonds — flowed up from Sparr's burning ship.

"They did it!" Julie gasped. "They got the diamonds!"

A moment later, Ro drifted into the glowing white moonlight and vanished.

"Hey, I almost forgot!" Eric said. "When Sparr was in the Tower of Memory, he read something at the very top. Then he said the word 'ice.'"

Galen frowned. "Some new evil that Sparr is planning against our world. You have done well, Eric. You have all done well. Time will tell what this clue means. But one thing is certain. Sparr's power is growing. Be watchful, be careful. . . ."

"Look! Look!" Max chirped from the backseat. "The rainbow-colored stairs are ahead!"

Khan swooped the ship into the Kalahar Valley. He pulled up to the shimmering staircase.

Eric, Julie, and Neal climbed out and onto the bottom step. They turned to Keeah.

"We'll be back," Eric told her. "Definitely."

Keeah looked into their eyes. "Droon is lucky to have friends like you. I am lucky to have such friends."

"Any day," said Neal. "Anytime."

"Anywhere the stairs lead us," Julie added.

Keeah smiled. "The magic is with us all!"

The kids waved good-bye as Khan's purple wingship circled the rainbow stairs and flew up into the clouds.

The three friends ran up the steps and into the small room at the top. Then they turned once more to the midnight sky of Droon.

The fierce wind had died down.

Droon was at peace for a little while.

At least it seemed so.

Eric flicked the light switch on the wall.

Whoosh! The magic stairs vanished, and the gray cement floor was beneath them again.

Neal opened the door and they stepped out into the basement. The clock on the workbench had hardly moved at all. They had been gone only a few minutes.

"It seems like we've been in Droon for years," Eric said. He glanced back at the small door under the basement steps.

"I'm really tired," Neal said, yawning. "But I can't wait to go back. You might even say I'm *itching* to go back!"

Julie chuckled. "Me, too. I hope it will be soon. Maybe we'll actually stop Sparr. Maybe we'll help Keeah find her mother. That would be so cool!"

"Maybe," said Eric as they headed upstairs to the kitchen. Then he remembered Galen's words.

Be watchful, be careful. . . .

Eric shivered when he thought of all the bad things that might happen.

He felt cold somehow.

As cold as . . . ice.